ABOUT THE AUTHOR

Dave Eggers is the author of many books, including *The Captain and the Glory*; *The Monk of Mokha*; *Your Fathers, Where Are They? And the Prophets, Do They Live Forever?*, shortlisted for the International Dublin Literary Award; *A Hologram for the King*, a finalist for the National Book Award; and *What is the What*, a finalist for the National Book Critics Circle Award and winner of France's Prix Médicis Étranger. He is the founder of McSweeney's Publishing and the co-founder of Voice of Witness, a book series that uses oral history to illuminate human rights crises. In 2002 he co-founded 826 Valencia, a youth writing centre with a pirate-supply storefront, which has inspired similar programmes around the world. ScholarMatch, now ten years old, connects donors with students to make college possible for all. In 2018 Dave Eggers co-founded the International Congress of Youth Voices, a global gathering of writers and activists under twenty. He is a winner of the Dayton Literary Peace Prize and the Muhammad Ali Humanitarian Award, and is a member of the American Academy of Arts and Letters.

www.internationalcongressofyouthvoices.org
www.internationalallianceofyouthwritingcenters.org
www.826national.org
www.826valencia.org
www.scholarmatch.org
www.voiceofwitness.org
www.valentinoachakdeng.org
www.mcsweeneys.net
www.daveeggers.net

Also by Dave Eggers

FICTION

Heroes of the Frontier
Your Fathers, Where Are They? And the Prophets, Do They
  Live Forever?
The Circle
A Hologram for the King
What is the What
How We are Hungry
You Shall Know Our Velocity!

MEMOIR

A Heartbreaking Work of Staggering Genius

NON-FICTION

The Monk of Mokha
Understanding the Sky
Zeitoun

AS EDITOR

Surviving Justice: America's Wrongfully Convicted and Exonerated (with Dr Lola Vollen)
The Voice of Witness Reader: Ten Years of Amplifying Unheard Voices

FOR YOUNG READERS

The Wild Things
This Bridge Will Not Be Gray
Her Right Foot
The Lifters
What Can a Citizen Do?

THE
PARADE

a novel

DAVE EGGERS

PENGUIN BOOKS

PENGUIN BOOKS

UK | USA | Canada | Ireland | Australia
India | New Zealand | South Africa

Penguin Books is part of the Penguin Random House group of companies
whose addresses can be found at global.penguinrandomhouse.com.

First published in the United States of America by Alfred A. Knopf 2019
First published in Great Britain by Hamish Hamilton 2019
Published in Penguin Books 2020
001

Printed and bound in Great Britain by Clays Ltd, Elcograf S.p.A.

A CIP catalogue record for this book is available from the British Library

ISBN: 978-0-241-98627-1

www.greenpenguin.co.uk

MIX
Paper from
responsible sources
FSC® C018179

Penguin Random House is committed to a
sustainable future for our business, our readers
and our planet. This book is made from Forest
Stewardship Council® certified paper.

THE PARADE

I

IN THE MORNING'S platinum light he raised his leaden head. He was lying on a plastic mattress, in a converted shipping container, below a tiny fan that circulated the room's tepid air.

He washed himself with packaged towelettes and put on his uniform, a black jumpsuit of synthetic fiber. Under a quickly rising sun he walked across the hotel's gravel courtyard to his partner's room. They had never met. He knocked on the corrugated steel door. There was no answer. He knocked louder.

After some shuffling from within, a lithesome man answered, naked but for a pair of white boxers. He had dark eyes, a cleft chin and a wide mouth ringed with full, womanly lips. A swirl of black hair rakishly obscured his left eye.

"Pick a number."

"Nine," the man at the door said, smiling slyly.

"Okay. You know how the company handles names. I don't know yours, you don't know mine. For the next two weeks, you're Nine. Call me Four."

"You're Four?"

"You will call me Four. I'll call you Nine. Got it?"

For reasons of security, the company insisted on simple pseudonyms, usually numerical.

"Got it," Nine said, and swept his hair from his face and threw it back.

They had arrived without passports. Passports were complications and liabilities in such a place, a nation recovering from years of civil war, riddled with corruption and burdened now by a new and lawless government. Four and Nine had been flown in under assumed names on a private charter. In the past, in other nations, the company's employees had been ransomed and killed. The kidnappers went first for their quarry's company, then family, then nation. But without passports or names, men like Four and Nine were anonymous and of little value. Their machine, the RS-80, was almost impossible to trace. It bore no company name, no serial number and had no national registry. No one but their clients, the northern government in the capital, would know anything about them, their origins or employer.

"You ready to eat?" Four asked. "We have forty minutes till we begin. The crew is making a final check on the machine."

"Soon," Nine said, a smile overtaking his expansive mouth. Nine stepped out of the doorway and tilted his head toward the bed behind him.

Beyond Nine's naked torso Four could see the furrowed sheets of an unmade bed, and woven within them the muscular legs of a sleeping woman. Nine made no effort to hide her. Instead he smiled conspiratorially. Four had never met this man, and did not think himself capable of prophecy, but in an instant he knew Nine was an agent of chaos and would make the difficult work ahead far more so.

Now Nine yawned. "Can I meet you in a few minutes?"

Four closed the door and made his way across the courtyard, now baking in the day's young heat, to the cafeteria. The room was humid with men bent over their food—men in suits, men in faded military uniforms, men in traditional dress. All spoke in low voices over the clacking of cheap tin silverware on plastic plates.

There were only a few foreigners in the makeshift dining hall attached to this new hotel, comprising two dozen

5

shipping containers arranged in an untidy semicircle. After waiting half an hour in the breakfast room, Four went to Nine's room again and knocked on the door.

"Coming!" Nine yelled, and the room burst with laughter.

Four returned to the cafeteria and drank bottled water. Ten minutes later Nine entered the room, having showered and dressed in his company-issued black jumpsuit. He had, though, declined to insert himself into the suit's upper half. He wore a white V-neck undershirt, the jumpsuit's sleeves dangling limply by his side, petting the other men's shoulders as he slipped around the tables on his way to Four.

"I didn't expect you here today," Nine said. "The planes in these parts aren't so punctual. That's why I had company last night. You married?"

"No," Four lied.

"You're not eating?" Nine asked.

"I already ate," Four said. In his room, he had finished a packet of dry oatmeal and powdered milk, a bag of almonds and a length of venison jerky—all of which he had brought with him. He had packed enough food for the twelve days the job was expected to take.

"You ate in your *room*?" Nine said, offended. "You can't do *that*. The food here's so good. Well, it's not so good, but it's *intriguing*." His hair had fallen over his left eye and he flung it back with a flourish of his hand.

"I'll get to it," Nine said, and went to the buffet and chose half a grapefruit, a tall glass of mango juice, three boiled eggs and a few shards of animal bone covered in purple meat. On his way back to the table, Nine's lifeless sleeves again flailed amid the other diners. Four looked around the room to see if any of the local men, a mix of former rebel commanders and recent profiteers, had taken an interest in Four or Nine. None had. He and his new partner were obviously foreigners in a place where most visitors were aid workers and arms inspectors, and it was better if they remained unmemorable.

Nine set his plate down and allowed his hair to fall from his forehead like the tendrils of a willow. Eschewing the tin utensils, Nine used his fingers to bring the gamey bones to his mouth for gnawing and washed the meat down with sun-colored juice. The company had advised against eating regional fruit in whole or liquid form, and strongly suggested that eggs or meat could contain *E. coli,* salmonella or ringworm. But Nine was devouring it all with abandon, his greasy hair groping his plate obscenely. Four could not discern what the company saw in this man. He was a liability.

"You know what she cost?" Nine asked, his mouth

full. He did not wait for Four to answer. "Less than what we're paying for breakfast. And she was fresher than this," he said, jabbing his fork at the wet grapefruit before him.

"The machine's waiting," Four said. "The first pod is in place. How long until you're ready?"

Nine looked at him, grinning. "Now I know why they call you the Clock."

Four stood. "Be ready in ten minutes," he said.

"You're not serious. I just got in yesterday," Nine said. "The schedule's padded. This is a great town. Let's spend a day here. Another night, more importantly." He raised an eyebrow lewdly. "I'll loan you my girl."

Four pushed in his chair. "I'll meet you out front in ten minutes. Bring all your gear."

II

"GET IN," FOUR said. He was sitting in a taxi, waiting in the hotel roundabout. Nine had just left the lobby, carrying his duffel bag and wearing sandals, looking like a tourist embarking on a day's excursion. He got in and the taxi took off.

"You'll have to change your shoes," Four said.

Nine opened his mouth, tilted his head like an animal and then smiled, as if deciding among many witty things he might say. He said nothing. Again he flung the hair back from his forehead.

Four knew this sort of man, a man amused by everything, most of all himself. He had grown his hair in such a way that it impeded his vision and had to be pushed out of the way a hundred times a day. It was nonsense. For a man so disposed, this job was an adventure, a lark.

But Four did not want to be here any longer than

was necessary. The humidity, even on the drive from the airport to the city, was an affliction. He knew that while suffering in this kind of heat he would be alternately catatonic and quick to anger. But inside the cab of the RS-80, there would be air-conditioning, and the assignment was simple. They were to pave and paint 230 kilometers of a two-lane roadway, uniting the country's rural south to the country's capital in the urban north.

The corridor had been cleared and the road had been graded and compacted. But the rainy season would come soon, and if the road went unpaved, all that work would quickly wash away. Four had studied the plans and had seen the road on the satellite pictures. He had never worked on a road so straight. It cut through scrub and desert and forests and villages, but all along there were no hills or mountains or cities. It was almost entirely unimpeded.

"So you've worked a lot of jobs," Nine said. He'd adopted a respectful, earnest tone, but the guise was ill fitting. Again the beginnings of a smile overtook his feminine mouth.

"This is my sixty-third assignment," Four said. He left it there. In eight years he had paved over seventy-five hundred kilometers on four continents.

"You seen any trouble?" Nine asked.

Four had been held at gunpoint only twice. Work like his often took place near the time and place of violence and atrocities without actually intersecting with either. On previous jobs, Four had seen what he later learned was a passenger plane falling from the sky, shot down by a surface-to-air missile. He had passed wells poisoned with corpses. He once missed by minutes the scene of a crucifixion. "No," he answered.

"You've used this machine before?" Nine asked.

"I have," Four said.

This was not strictly true. This was his first field assignment with this particular vehicle. It was only the second time the company had used the RS-80, a significant improvement over its previous incarnation, the RS-50. Among other changes, the cockpit of the new model accommodated only one person. The RS-50 had room for two, and sharing the small cockpit had driven Four to distraction. Only one person was necessary inside and the new model rightfully recognized this. For this assignment, the company determined that the second crew member would drive a quad, a four-wheeled all-terrain vehicle, to scout ahead for obstructions and to ensure that the pods were not tampered with. That would be Nine's purview.

"Check it out," Nine said, and pointed to the side of

the muddy road. Four wasn't sure what Nine had found interesting. None of this was new. Everything around them was standard for a developing country after a war. The soda bottles full of diesel, lined up on the roadside and sold by shrunken grandmothers. The stray dogs and children holding babies. The diagonal plumes of faraway fires. The spent rifle shells. The teenagers wearing mirrored sunglasses and carrying unloaded AKs. The trucks delivering glittering things unseen for years in the region—air conditioners, file cabinets, undefiled windows, even stained glass for some foreign-funded church. The white trucks full of aid workers fretful or debauched.

All around were scenes of reconstruction. On a rickety scaffolding made of gnarled sticks, a dozen masons were repairing a municipal building with a cloud-shaped hole in its façade. Next door a middle-aged woman, wearing a fur-lined winter coat, sat under a striped beach umbrella, next to an office copier that she'd somehow wheeled out onto the roadside. A line of men and women in business attire waited to avail themselves of her services. The high-pitched whine of a diesel scooter overtook them, and Nine laughed.

"Whole clan," he said.

Four glanced over to see that a family of five had arranged themselves on one small scooter, and soon passed them and swung into their lane. Two of the children were standing on the runner in front of their father, whose wife clung tight to him with a baby strapped to her back. The baby, fast asleep and its face cloudy with diesel fumes, wore a stocking cap covered with jewels and bells.

This was a burgeoning city awake and alive after a civil war its residents assumed would have no end. All the glass had been shattered, all the roofs caved in, there were legless men and clinics full of the dying and destitute. There were a million displaced, a million in exile, ten thousand orphans. And yet everyone was jubilant amid the construction, amid the unmanaged garbage, the waste dumped into local streams, the sweeping shoals of bright plastic bottles everywhere. Amid the chaos there was joy and frenetic enterprise. There was a rush of foreign aid, reconstruction funds, foreigners coming to assess and consult, to hand out grants and bribes and collect fees. Homes became hotels; kitchens became restaurants. The visitors needed bottled water, soda, whiskey, chicken, candy, beef. Land a meal for six aid workers and pay your family's way for a month. Or buy a scooter to carry your family away.

"We'll work a long day today," Four said. "Get ahead of the schedule while we can." As he spoke the words, he knew Nine would suppress a private smile, and indeed he did. Four looked away from him and caught sight of a pair of men unloading a new dishwasher from an oxcart that also contained an elderly woman on a gurney, an IV rigged above her via duct tape and a cricket bat.

The two of them had twelve days to complete the work. The RS-80 had been designed to pave 25 kilometers a day, but could be pushed to 30. Four expected the 230 kilometers to be finished in ten days. Still, the company had built in a small cushion, two days, for any eventualities. The company would receive a bonus from the government if the schedule was kept, so every extra day threatened the schedule, which threatened the company's bonus, which threatened Four's compensation.

Most crucial, the road had to be finished in time for the parade. The president, known for political theater, had planned for the parade to begin the moment the road was completed. The procession would leave the capital and travel south, symbolizing an end to decades of war and the beginning of the peace and prosperity the road would make possible.

The RS-80 reduced any doubt about meeting such a compressed schedule. Given they were paving during the dry season, no rain was plausible, and outside of rain, there were virtually no variables. When there were no variables and no distractions, Four could be counted on to complete any job on time or early. Beyond sleep and an occasional meal, Four did not rest while on assignment. He did not take breaks unless they were unavoidable.

"You been here before?" Nine asked.

"No," Four said. He watched as Nine flung his hair from his eyes again and ran his hand over the totality of his skull. Soon the hair he'd just moved out of the way impeded his vision again. Preposterous, Four thought.

"This is your first assignment," Four said.

"Yes," Nine said.

"You understand your role?"

"Yes. Clear the road, *mitigate obstacles.*" Nine uttered the last two words with a tone of mock formality.

Four gave him a hard stare and took a breath. Their taxi passed a pair of police officers lounging in the back of a pickup truck, their legs latticed and feet bare. A line of schoolchildren walked by wearing khaki pants and bright white shirts and carrying books donated by some distant government. A flatbed truck sped by conveying a small mountain of bent and burned steel.

"Your job is to drive ahead with the quad and make sure nothing is on the road as I approach. Not a person. Not an animal. Nothing. Small rocks are fine. If you see deep grooves, you need to tell me. If you see a cavity, a tear, anything unusual, you inform me. Okay?"

"Yes."

"You especially need to keep other vehicles off the surface. You need to clear cars, motorcycles, goats, cattle, bikes, anything heavy. A loaded cart or truck might rut the road and make the surface uneven. You understand?"

"Yes."

"Some surface variation is acceptable, and almost inevitable in a place like this, but your task is to reduce these variations, which means reducing the number of vehicles and anything else using or crossing the road. Yes?"

"Yes."

"If you find a significant surface variation, you are tasked with filling it in before the RS-80 arrives, and if the variation is too large to fix, you will have to radio me, or come back to me in person. Then we can assess whether we power down to fix the anomaly, or if we just pave over it. Okay?"

"Okay."

"When I'm halfway to the next pod," Four continued, "you go and check to be sure there is nothing and no one near that pod. The pods are curiosities to people, but they are everything to us. They contain the asphalt and the RS-80's fuel. If even one is tampered with, our work ends.

It was exceedingly difficult for the company to get all the pods here. You understand?"

"I do."

"Even though they're too heavy for anyone to lift, and sensors will tell us if any pod is molested, your job is to make sure there's no one even near the next pod. No one touching it, sitting on top of it. Nothing like that. Got it?"

"Right. Clear obstacles, human and nonhuman. And no molesting." Again Nine smiled as if he'd made a joke. Realizing that Four was not a receptive audience, Nine leaned into the window separating the back seat from the front, and, to the surprise of Four and the taxi driver, unleashed a stream of sentences in the regional dialect. Four remembered now that Nine's profile had indicated he could speak the local tongue; it was one of the few qualifications he seemed to possess.

As they left the city and while Nine and the taxi driver carried on a spirited conversation, the makeshift shops and hotels gave way to shanties and piles of burning garbage. At the outskirts of town, through a veil of orange dust, Four could see where the road began. The RS-80 rested beside it, a low-slung machine painted a dull yellow and trimmed in black. Four had been assured that this machine was almost new, used only once, and even then for fewer than ten kilometers of roadway.

Nine pointed to it, and he and the taxi driver spoke excitedly. Nine turned back to Four. "He says he worked on a road crew once. He says he doesn't believe this one machine does everything itself."

Four got out of the taxi and paid the driver. It was half past 8:00 a.m., the sun already high above the tree line. He marked the time in his notebook and walked toward the paver. Four watched as Nine lingered at the taxi driver's window, finishing with an elaborate handshake and an uproarious laugh. "No no no!" he roared to the driver, and jogged to catch up with Four.

III

IN THE PAST, paving a road like this would require the labor of at least four vehicles and twelve people. It was messy and toxic work. From a distance, the process had looked like a very slow and disorganized circus. A sixteen-wheel dump truck would drive backward, its bed lifted, pouring hot asphalt into the paver's great funnel, which would then apply it to the road. Later, a roller would follow, compacting the surface and making it uniform. Workers, walking alongside, had to be present to ensure the smooth execution of every step.

But the RS-80 consolidated all of these tasks into an infinitely more efficient and elegant system. Instead of the asphalt being brought to the site by trucks, it was stored on the road in simple yellow pods, each about two meters square—they looked like enormous cubes with rounded corners, like unnumbered dice. Each pod would heat the asphalt via remote control, ensuring the mixture was ready when the RS-80 reached it. The RS-80 then would lift the pod until it locked into place atop the paver. The paver would then drink from it as it blackened the next ten kilometers. The work previously requiring a messy cluster of vehicles and people could now be done by one person in one machine.

Thus Four was dubious about the utility of Nine. Obstacles were unlikely, and satellite photography could find any notable impediments. In terms of human interference, certainly a factor in some areas of the world, all company research indicated this particular project had no local opposition. The road had been in the works for eighteen months, and regional support was unqualified. In the months leading up to Four's arrival, his colleagues had cleared the land and graded the road, and all the while, the locals had helped, whether paid for their work or not. When homes needed to be displaced, the locals made no argument; they accepted relocation stipends and left promptly. Given the scarcity of possessions in the average regional home, vacating usually took less than an hour.

Now the road was finished but for the paving, which was essential in land like this, prone to flooding. Until recently, most of the roads in this southern part of the country had been dirt paths, almost useless during the rains. Once this road was paved, all manner of goods from the northern capital could easily flow to the provinces—medicines and agricultural machinery and construction materials, all of which had been scarce until now. Before this road, the drive from the capital to the rest of the country had taken four days at best, and along the way there were no fuel stations, no one to repair a vehicle. The buses that traveled the route had to bring their own gas, which made them easy targets for bandits. This new road would bring safety and progress to the provinces at seventy miles an hour. The remote areas of the south would leap forward a hundred years in a matter of months.

The road began in a nondescript construction area on the outskirts of the city. A motley array of aging vehicles, loaders and diggers and graders, stood unmanned around what would someday be the on-ramp to the highway. An enormous new billboard recommended infant immunizations.

The RS-80 had been delivered the day before but its lower half was already coated in a film of red dust. Two figures in blue jumpsuits were moving quickly around it. The vehicle had been transported by barge and overland by truck, and wherever it was being transported so far, mechanics had to accompany it and keep it ready until put to use. Aside from the two mechanics, there was no one near. Occasionally, at the beginning of an assignment, there would be dignitaries and fanfare, but the company felt, and Four agreed, that the work was best conducted with little attention.

Next to the RS-80 was a quad, relatively new. It was painted the same yellow as the paver, and was lined with black and chrome trim.

"This is mine?" Nine asked, and threw his leg over the seat.

"You've driven one of these?" Four asked.

Nine chuckled, said, "Of course," then scanned the controls like a cat following an elusive string. Knowing he was being watched, he abandoned the task and addressed the helmet on the rear of the quad. Throwing his head back to set his hair in the proper position, he put the helmet on with great care, then continued to examine the machine, having no idea how to start it.

"We'll leave in a few minutes," Four told him, and followed the two mechanics around the RS-80 for a final inspection.

A shoeless man in a rumpled suit approached quickly,

holding a filthy hand to his mouth as if feeding himself an invisible morsel. Four said nothing to him and did not look into his face. He turned his attention to the machine, seeing only the man's broken toenails in the dust. The mechanics too knew how to behave. They assiduously avoided the man's entreaties, and went about their work. In seconds the man understood their point of view and the futility in pursuing them, and moved on to Nine, who immediately unsettled the natural order. He took off his helmet and looked into the man's eyes. He made a show of slapping his pockets, indicating he had no cash or food for the man. The man, having achieved such significant engagement, now made his feeding gesture more dramatically, as if a more heightened performance would produce food or money in Nine. Nine looked Four's way, knowing he had created a problem. Four and the mechanics moved to the far side of the machine, continuing their inspection and leaving Nine to solve the puzzle he'd begun.

The machine was in excellent shape and was fully fueled. Four and the mechanics shook hands and they left. They would be flying out that day, back to the company's regional hub. Four walked around the vehicle, examining the improvements made upon the RS-50. Everything, it seemed, had been both streamlined and strengthened. He ran his palm along the body of the machine, reveling in its solidity, its impenetrable exterior. The intake ramp was now shorter, more efficient. The loading mechanism was a work of art. And this model could paint, too. The government wanted a double yellow line down the entirety of the highway, and because the new bitumen dried almost immediately, it could be painted by the RS-80 without breaking stride.

The engine was running when Four stepped into the vehicle, taking in the smell of fresh plastic and new leather. It was spacious but everything was within reach. A key opened the dash, which revealed a series of compartments, all of them needing their own key to access. One compartment held detailed topographical maps in case the GPS failed. One held an elaborate toolkit for basic repairs. One held duplicate batteries, sparkplugs, caps and various bolts, filters and tubes. One held the satellite phone and kept it charged; there was no cell-phone reception in most of the country.

Under the seat a steel box contained a handgun, a sawed-off shotgun, two grenades, enough local currency to buy off a few villages and six cyanide packets. Four marked in his notebook that everything was in its place.

"Should I head out?" Nine said. He had appeared

at the window, though Four had already retracted the machine's steps.

"Are you standing on the chassis?" Four asked.

"Chassis?" Nine said, looking down. "I guess so."

"Don't stand there," Four said. Nine hopped down onto the road. "And don't engage with the locals. You know this. Now go. Ride the shoulder and look for impediments. Then fix them. Come back to me only when there's something you can't mitigate yourself."

"Got it," Nine said, and loped to the quad.

Four guided the RS-80 onto the roadbed. The first pod had been set up ten meters ahead, and he needed that distance to allow the machine's positioning system to get fully calibrated.

Now that the RS-80 was moving, a small crowd of local men appeared and watched the machine from a distance. Some wore traditional clothing and some wore athletic sweat suits. One man wore a battered and dusty tuxedo jacket with shorts and sandals. Because the RS-80 moved slowly, just above a human's walking pace, the men could stroll next to it without exertion.

Four looked to Nine, who was sitting on his quad, appearing prepared but not yet wearing his helmet. Four gave him a signal indicating they should be ready to begin, and hoped that Nine would put his helmet on and ride ahead as his assignment dictated. But instead Nine had struck up a conversation with the man in the tuxedo jacket.

Four felt a twinge of annoyance but instructed himself not to care. He put the RS-80 into gear, and the machine lurched forward. Four kilometers an hour was the vehicle's maximum speed, and though it was a miraculous rate for the finishing of a road, it was not a pace tolerable to all. Four found it meditative and the progress significant, but he had the distinct sense that Nine would not be satisfied with the machine's slow and deliberate speed.

The RS-80 reached the first pod and took it. A few locals stood fifty meters away, watching as the pod was pulled up the ramp, into the body of the paver, and locked into place. The vehicle continued, and the asphalt, already heated to three hundred degrees, began covering the road in a perfect black coat, the surface striped twice yellow but otherwise without blemish.

After a few hundred meters, the novelty of the machine had worn off for the locals, who turned and went on with their business. Women carrying groceries and firewood crossed the road behind the vehicle without any great fear of its heat or toxicity. They trusted Four, the machine and the expertise he, as a foreigner, represented. As Four passed the last kilometer of the city's outer ring, children waved but Four did not return their greetings. Four and his fellow operators had learned on uncountable previous assignments that any interaction, even a wave, was an invitation to conversation and complications. Some enterprising man would wave hello. Then he would signal the machine to stop, and if the driver were foolish enough to stop, the enterprising man would ask about employment, about ways he might help, about how he could ensure cooperation with the villages ahead. Bribes and delays would ensue.

The company assured its operators it was not impolite to look straight ahead, to concentrate only on the road, an extension of the machine. The locals would understand. In fact, they would have more respect for the drivers whose attention never wavered from the work at hand. It was important work, building a viable road. Nothing happening left or right mattered more.

A man seemed to be exercising, doing push-ups on the embankment. When Four drew closer, he realized the man's legs were withered or missing, his pant legs two shredded flags. The man was propelling himself forward by using his arms, which were scarred with severe burns, to drag his torso and legs along the gravel shoulder. Women and children walked by and offered no help and expressed no interest. It was not surprising to Four.

The beige city was soon behind him and the watchers were gone. Four checked the RS-80 systems, and all was optimal. Ahead, the clean diagonal lines of the road met at a tight point on the horizon. Once paved, the highway would be sublime.

IV

THE NEW COMPANY tents were designed to be
assembled quickly, and Four found it took less than
twenty seconds to convert the bundle of tubing and nylon
into a handsome red shelter, sturdy and commodious.

The day had been uneventful. He had paved
twenty-eight kilometers and the RS-80 was now parked
one meter away from the next pod. Nine had been reason-
ably helpful. All day he had ridden ahead and circled back
without news or concern. The road had been entirely free
of anomalies.

When Four shut down the RS-80, he'd sent Nine
ahead to make sure the next day's second pod was unmo-
lested. This was standard procedure, but Four was happy
to know he might relax for twenty minutes, alone, while
Nine traveled to tomorrow's pod, ten kilometers up the
road, and back.

With Nine out of sight, Four knelt on the asphalt and pressed his palms to its warm surface. It was exquisite. The new formula, created to reduce toxicity and to restrict cracking and cratering, was remarkable. Up close the road looked like silk. Four inhaled deeply, noting that the smell had been greatly diminished; its scent was now more like oatmeal than its previous, more industrial odor. The yellow double line was taut and already dry to the touch. The RS-80 had performed magnificently, Four would note in his report. Every so often, he thought, humans make a perfect machine, one that requires little maintenance, that efficiently draws what it needs from the world, executes its work and asks for nothing in return.

Four stood and took in the absolute quiet of his surroundings. He saw no settlements and heard no people. This was serenity, being alone with his road and the paver. It was the work at its essence; everything else was unnecessary. He had grown up on a farm and now lived on an island, and had come to know that the vast majority of the earth, its seas and plains and mountains, were empty and were silent. The natural condition of the world, its dominant state, was absolute quiet, and the illogical blessing of it all was that the creatures that make noise, the near totality of humanity, only want to be near more noise, leaving most of the planet vacant and serene.

Four unzipped his tent door and ducked inside, removing his boots before entering. His feet, freed, sighed and expanded and Four lay on his stomach. He opened his pack and removed and unrolled his sleeping bag and inflated his pillow. He retrieved from his pack another, heavier, nylon roll. Inside were three handguns and three knives. Two of the handguns were identical, capable of firing twelve rounds each from an automatic clip. He had eight of these clips, giving him ninety-six rounds. The third handgun was tiny, made of plastic, and was meant to be worn around the ankle and evade metal detectors. This gun could fire six rounds, all of the bullets plastic but able to penetrate wood, flesh or steel.

Four checked each gun for damage and found them to be in working condition. Of the three knives, the first was a large hunting knife, intended for hand-to-hand combat but also useful in dressing any animal he might need to kill for food. The second blade was smaller, and its handle shaped to fit around the knuckles. The third knife was simply a sturdy ceramic switchblade and could, like the plastic handgun, be easily concealed and was undetectable by the metal scanners used in the region.

Four left the largest and smallest knives in his tool roll and set the roll in a corner of the tent. The knuckled knife he put under his pillow. Likewise he hid the two guns; as was company policy, he set one of the handguns inside his sleeping bag.

It was rare for any of the company's workers to need to use any weapon, but it was important that the locals be aware that the employees were armed. Only on one occasion had Four reached for any weapon at all, and even then it was only to show his handgun to a would-be thief. This was three years prior, and the display of destructive power had had the desired effect.

By the time Four was finished arranging the interior of his tent, it was early evening. He was not hungry, but knew he should eat now, while there was light and while Nine was away. He returned to the RS-80 and set the water tank to boil. He went to his tent, retrieved a half-liter cup and filled it with hot water from the vehicle. He poured a packet of freeze-dried beef into the cup, and stirred it with his spoon. As it cooled, he installed his earphones and pressed play.

"Hey!" Nine's head appeared inside the tent, his hair covering his face. Four startled. "Sorry," Nine said, pushing back his hair to reveal his mirthful eyes. "Didn't mean to scare you." His smile retreated and he seemed unsure of which of his many tones and postures to adopt. Four looked at him, impassive. Nine cleared his throat.

"So I checked the next pod. Looked good. That is, it *appeared satisfactory*."

This was all said in what seemed to be Nine's most professional way. "You see all that crazy shit today? I assume you saw the cargo plane basically broken in half beside the road?"

Four had seen it.

"And the tank with the top of it just disappeared? You saw that fucking horse with the military, like, dressing on it, walking alone like some kind of tribute to a fallen hero? And you saw the electrical poles all along the road, and the crew setting them all up? I guess they'll be getting electricity down here the same time as they get a road."

Four had seen all of these things. He had seen the slanting smoke from distant rubber fires. The circling carrion birds. The stray dogs, the dead dogs. The pyramid of rusted bedframes. A shopping cart full of shattered mirrors. A pink bathrobe laid out carefully in the gravel. The ashes that had been homes. The schoolchildren in spotless yellow shirts walking to a school in a blue tent.

"And what's with all the black garbage bags?" Nine said. "There were hundreds of them by the road, in piles, right? It's like they're cleaning up and waiting for some kind of sanitation truck to come after us and pick it all up."

Seeing that Four had a bowl in his hand, Nine looked into it and winced. "What's that?" he asked, but didn't wait for the answer. "I can't eat that slop. Listen, I saw a place up ahead a ways. One of these micro-restaurants. Just a couple women cooking over an open fire, but it smelled spectacular. I can take us there."

Four swallowed a mouthful of his soupy mix. "We both need to stay here," he said. "Eating local food is strongly discouraged. You know this. It's in your contract."

"Can we at least eat outside?" Nine asked. "It's hot as fuck in here."

Four didn't move. He knew it was hot inside, but it was protocol to eat in one's tent. It eliminated potential curiosity or solicitations from locals. Four had no difficulty managing any heat or cold. He had worked in high winds, in sleet and snow and grisly heat. It was a matter of preparation and patience, given that all conditions were temporary. After each assignment, no matter what suffering he'd endured for a day or a week, he had gone home on time.

Nine's face retreated from the tent and he stood. Four could see that Nine seemed to be deciding what to do.

Now Nine crouched, his face visible in the tent door again and his eyes bright behind the dangling vines of his hair.

"I met a woman on the road today," he said, throwing his head back to free his eyes. "She waved to me and I stopped. Did you see any of the women? There's some stunning talent here, even when they're modestly dressed, right? Maybe especially that type, the supposedly demure and supplicating. They have a sexy way, right? There's allure in the enigma—the riddle of the hidden body but then the audacious eyes. It's like a sea at night, all black and unknown, but with a lighthouse screaming from above. Those eyes are always screaming *I want, I want!* You know what I mean. I know you do. And this one, she was really bold. She wanted to know when we'd be finished, and we talked about all the changes the road is bringing to the area. A lot's happening already—she was effusive about it."

Finished with his meal, Four wiped his bowl and utensils with a paper towel and set them back in his kit.

"You see how many businesses have already popped up?" Nine continued. "I counted a few hundred today already. You probably saw them. All those little restaurants and shops made with salvaged metal and plywood? Right now they're no more than shacks selling a few

35

things, but it's microenterprise. It's self-determination, growth. Did you see the beauty shop?"

Four assumed the question was rhetorical, and ignored it until the silence implied Nine wanted an answer.

"No," Four said.

"The New World Beauty Emporium? With the hand-painted sign and all the headless mannequins out front?"

Four said nothing.

"These businesses," Nine went on breathlessly, "they're a way to ensure some kind of peace. The more people are invested in their own enterprise, the more they're building something, are rooted and growing, the less likely they'll be to accept war as a solution—to be taken in by one of these rebel opportunists. Not that they could do much anyway now. Apparently as part of the peace agreement, the rebels gave up all their heavy artillery, their few planes and tanks. It sounded like a one-sided arrangement if you ask me."

Nine's hair had dropped in front of his eyes, and Four knew it was time for Nine to throw it back again. He watched, fascinated by the predictability of Nine, his clownishness. But Nine mistook Four's sociological curiosity for genuine interest in his blatherings, and grew more expansive.

"But I have to say, I feel so full here. The people's optimism is like the birth of a star. It's incandescent. My heart is full. Is your heart full?" Four said nothing and Nine seemed to take his silence for agreement. "Yeah," he continued, "I don't know if I've ever felt so immediately and profoundly connected. They know me. They look at me, they see me, they acknowledge me in a way no one ever has. At the same time, I know and they know that I am nothing but that I am listening. That I care. And so what we do here matters even though I don't personally matter."

Four checked his watch. It was seven o'clock. He needed to write a summary of the day's work for the company, and that would take him to 7:40. Then he had to do a thorough check on the RS-80. That would take him to 8:10 or so. Then he needed to wind down before bed. He wanted to be asleep by 9:20 p.m. for a 6:00 a.m. start.

"You're always looking at your watch," Nine said. "Thus the name the Clock."

"No one calls me the Clock."

Nine blinked quickly, surprised to be corrected.

"I'm sorry. I actually thought it was a nickname you liked."

"It's not. No one's ever called me that."

Nine paused, as if formulating and discarding a half-dozen rejoinders. For a moment his face was tense with the sentences not said, and finally relaxed when he had forsaken them all for silence. He took a deep breath and began again. "The road is a highway of life, don't you see? Like a mighty tree. And all these homes and businesses opening alongside, they're like roots extending from the tree, digging in, drawing life from the tree, creating opportunity and, from that, stability."

Four looked at his shoes. If he had to endure this kind of chatter every night he would go mad.

"Don't you ever stop and feel good about any of this?" Nine asked.

Four thought that perhaps he had made an error in preventing Nine from seeking his dinner elsewhere. With Nine gone, Four could eat and work in silence. Then again, if he allowed Nine to eat at some roadside shack, he was risking Nine getting sick, and that would mean delays and a compromised schedule.

"I have to write my report," Four said. "Have a good dinner." Four retrieved his log and began filling it out.

Four heard Nine walk for a time outside, his steps loud on the road's gravel shoulder. There was nothing useful Nine could be doing out there. There was no reason to be tramping around so loudly. Finally Four zipped his tent closed.

"Nice night out here," Nine said from the other side of the nylon. He began whistling some tuneless dirge.

Four put his earphones in and pressed play. In half an hour he finished his report and was ready to do his check on the RS-80. He was about to leave the tent when Nine unzipped Four's tent door and inserted his face yet again.

"I know I shouldn't have, but I brought a little something." He held aloft a flask. "Got it in the city before we left. Want some?"

"No," Four said. "You shouldn't have that."

Nine forced his face into a faux-sheepish expression and tucked the flask into his jumpsuit.

"What are you listening to?" Nine asked.

Four said nothing. It was evident that Nine had already been drinking. It must have been some kind of bathtub moonshine; his medicinal breath filled the tent. Again Four instructed himself to keep his anger in check. In the thirty-six hours Nine had been in the city alone, this man had hired at least one prostitute and had found alcohol where it was strictly prohibited. Now he had reentered Four's tent uninvited, having quickly brought himself to intoxication.

"Remember that woman you saw me with this morning? She was actually pretty. Her ass was like two basketballs, inflated just right. 'Ever let the Fancy roam, / Pleasure never is at home.' You know that one? My bastard father made us all recite poetry."

Nine paused, as if expecting Four to ask him about this fascinating piece of Nine's history, his being made to recite poetry by a bastard father. When Four made no inquiry, Nine seemed momentarily surprised but pressed on.

"That's the thing about this part of the world—the prostitutes aren't strung-out bags of pus. They're fresh, unspoiled. 'She will mix these pleasures up / Like three fit wines in a cup.' You have to know that one! Same poem, actually."

No man, Four thought, should have to endure another man quoting poetry and asking the listener to guess from what dead author it came.

"My lady had long hair, and it smelled like wool, but in other places she smelled so sweet." Seeing no reaction from Four, he pushed on. "Her bush was delicious. I know most men won't drink from a whore's bush but I love it. I always love it. She was amazed I'd do it. She spread her legs and let me feast."

"Get out of here," Four said.

Nine seemed to think he was joking, that Four was enjoying his story. "I'm not one to mistake a whore's kindness for love or even affection," he continued, "but this lady was different. I think she was grateful for me paying her enough that she could sleep all night in one bed. We were *both* grateful. She was grateful, and that made her kind, and I was grateful for her kindness. When you knocked on the door we'd just finished another go, and it was genuinely tender—like we had a real understanding about the mutual benefit of giving each other pleasure. You ever feel that with a pro?"

Four briefly pictured beating Nine senseless with his fists.

"No," Four said, and threw the tent flap closed.

THE HEAT HAD not let up during the night. At dawn
Four woke up in a tight cocoon of sweat and dust.

V

THE HEAT HAD not let up during the night. At dawn
Four woke up in a tight cocoon of sweat and dust.

He stood, stretched, opened his tent to a pearly sky
and relieved himself on the side of the road. From the
RS-80 he filled a jerrican with water and, standing on
the new road, now paved and cooled, he cleaned himself.
Afterward he could still smell his human stink, so he
went to his tent, retrieved his supply bag, opened a
packet of sanitizing towelettes and cleaned himself a
second time. Eventually the smell faded.

He checked the time. Six thirty-seven. He turned
on the RS-80's computer and activated the first pod. It
would take thirty minutes to heat, so they would need to
begin moving in twenty. But Nine had not appeared from
his tent.

"Twenty minutes," Four said in the direction of Nine's tent. He heard no response. He tapped the vinyl cover.

"Yes, who is it?" Nine said in a comic falsetto.

"Twenty minutes," Four said.

Four unwrapped a nutrition bar and ate it while standing on the road. He looked back on the road he'd paved the day before. It was immaculate and black and its perfection gave him an inner click of satisfaction. He filled his thermos with clean water from the RS-80, drank half of it down, swallowed a handful of vitamins and began disassembling his tent. When he was finished and had stuffed the tent in the RS-80's side compartment, Nine emerged from his tent.

"Good day, sir," he said, and bowed.

"Twelve minutes," Four said.

"You eat yet?" Nine asked. "Actually, I don't want to know. The way you eat is so fucking depressing. They gave me some eggs last night. Want one?"

"Last night?" Four said. "Who gave you eggs?"

"Oh. Oh Jesus. How to explain? How. To. Explain? After you went to sleep, your belly full of your robot food, I went to that village we passed a ways back and I had real sustenance. The paver can boil water, right? Saved two for you." He had two eggs in his hands, and

43

walked to the RS-80. He found the water tank and set it to boil.

"That's not for boiling eggs," Four said, but he knew that Nine would not be dissuaded. "How did you get there?"

Nine leaned against the vehicle and scratched his groin. "So you were asleep at what, nine or ten? I didn't want to wake you, so I didn't start up the quad. I set out on foot, just going back on the road we already paved, and Jesus Christ, I've never seen so many stars. Incredible sky here. It's so close, like you could jump up and wave your hands and gather the stars like sand. So I walked with my head thrown back, just astonished, and all along I would encounter people, and when they saw my jump-suit they knew I was part of the road team. And they were so thankful. So grateful. I mean, they were walking on the surface barefoot, the asphalt still warm, just to see what it felt like! These people had never really seen a properly paved road."

The water boiled, and Nine dropped the eggs in. "So I made it to the village, just following the road, right? And it was lit up, just strung with single bulbs, holiday lights. It was alive. We passed it during the day, and then it just looked like a series of shanties, right? But walking through it at night—god, it was so awake, so electric. People everywhere. They were surprised to see me, because there's absolutely no one here like us, but after a while I was just another fact of their lives. There was music coming from tiny radios and boom boxes from another age, machines I hadn't seen in twenty years. CDs, cassettes even! So much music. And the food!"

Nine offered Four a boiled egg he'd peeled.

"No," Four said. "Two minutes till we leave."

Nine ate the eggs in a rush of ravenous swallows. "Oh, these are so good. Laid just yesterday. This woman took them from the chicken's roost. Grabbed them right from under the hen's ass. I watched her. Oh, Jesus. They taste like life."

Nine ate with his eyes closed, swallowing the last of the embryos. His tent was still assembled. Four realized that it would take ten minutes for Nine to get his gear together. He wouldn't be able to get it into the storage compartment before Four needed to get the RS-80 moving.

"You'll have to carry your stuff on the quad," Four said. "I'm leaving on time."

"That's fine," Nine said. "I'll catch up to you in a second, and maybe at lunch I can tell you about the special lady I met last night. It's a sweet story, I promise, very chaste. But the way she danced—" He did a vague imitation of a woman's swaying hips and lewdly ran his hands over his own waist.

Four checked his watch, knowing the RS-80 would thrum momentarily, which it did, indicating that the first pod was hot. "Be quick," he told Nine. He stepped up into the RS-80 and closed the door.

VI

IT WAS TWENTY minutes before Nine appeared on his quad, waving as he shot by on the road's shoulder in a tantrum of pink dust. He was not wearing his helmet, and his arms were exposed in a region known for malaria. His speed was excessive and his wake clouded the air with an unnecessary red fog. He had packed his tent haphazardly on the back of the quad. When he passed, Four could see little through the dust but Nine's wide smile, the look of a teenager tearing down a beach on a borrowed machine.

Between this and the visit to the village last night, Four considered using the satellite phone to call headquarters to request a replacement for Nine. But he knew that would alert them to a problem. The company referred to such a problem, to any problem, as an anomaly, and anomalies reflected badly on everyone involved. The driver's job was to mitigate anomalies and keep the schedule. On Four's first assignment, thinking he was being thorough, he had reported a series of anomalies the first day, and was gently told that though his attention to detail was appreciated, the company did not need to know about ruts, divots, grooves or questions posed by local citizens. Four was expected to handle these issues and keep moving. Anomalies were to be solved, not reported.

Four decided he would speak to Nine at lunch. Normally he would not take a full lunch on the second day of an assignment, but in this case he had to make an exception. With this man he needed to set parameters. To calm himself, he put his earphones in and pressed play.

The road presented no issues throughout the morning. Four passed more of the black garbage bags, more of the electrical poles ready to be erected and wired. He saw small settlements on either side and occasional evidence of homes that had been moved or disassembled to make way for the new highway. He had been warned that some of the forests had been mined during the war and saw, midmorning, warning signs nailed to trees, skulls and crossbones and plaintive words in the local tongue.

Ahead Four could see the next pod, a half kilometer

away, and from this distance he could see that there appeared to be people sitting or standing on top of it. This, the clearing of locals from the road and particularly from the pods, was the work Nine was hired to do. But he was nowhere in sight.

When Four was close enough to make out the figures, he saw that it was a trio of boys playing on the pod. Four lowered his window and waved his arm, motioning the boys to get off. When they jumped down, they were immediately admonished by a pair of women, who grabbed the boys' arms roughly and pulled them away from the road. When Four reached the pod, the RS-80 took it into its docking bay and drank from it without incident.

But when Four looked in the rearview mirror, he saw Nine had caught up with him, and now was surrounded by the same boys. They were touching the quad and Nine was allowing it. Nine produced a camera, and began taking pictures of the boys. One of the boys was wearing a purple scarf, though the temperature was soaring. Each time Nine took a picture, he would show the boys the photo on his viewscreen, and they would all laugh. It seemed the boys had not seen such a camera before, one that could show the image immediately after taking it. Four thought about retrieving Nine, but that would mean interrupting their party and being inevitably drawn into it.

Four stayed in the vehicle and started the engine, planning to eat his lunch in the moving cab. As the vehicle lurched forward, Nine looked up, perplexed. Four made no gesture to explain. He would have his discussion with Nine that night. He resolved then that it would be a more serious talk than the one he'd planned for lunch.

Nine did not appear again until the midafternoon, when he came hurtling up the shoulder, now shirtless and wearing the purple scarf that Four had seen on the boy. In company briefings, all transactions were discouraged, whether they involved barter or cash. The locals could easily claim that the scarf had been stolen, and this increased the likelihood of interaction with unreliable local authorities. Nine swerved up the embankment and rode parallel to the RS-80, smiling broadly, trying to catch Four's eye. Four did not turn to him, and Nine rode on ahead, his hand in the air, waving to the world in his wake.

VII

BY LATE AFTERNOON, Four had paved twenty-eight kilometers and the machine needed rest. Four powered down and found a level spot near the road for his tent. He could hear the faint sounds of far-off singing—a group of voices rising and falling in harmony. The sky was a flat white.

Four set up his tent and sleeping bag and pillow, and laid his head upon it. The distant music was pleasant and he wondered about its provenance. It sounded like a chorus of some kind, perhaps religious, the voices all female, he guessed. He put his earphones in and pressed play, closing his eyes and making plans. He wanted to talk to Nine over dinner, but after waiting twenty minutes, he got up and began making his meal alone.

He ate a packet of crackers, two nutrition bars, a large bag of nuts and a handful of vitamins as the faraway music stopped and then began again, this time louder. What had been a shy chorus was now bolder, wilder. Four was curious about the music and where it was coming from. If he were at home, Four might seek out its source, but he couldn't leave the RS-80 unattended. He finished his meal at 5:15.

He went into his tent to check on his tools. He unrolled his pack and removed the plastic pistol, briefly cleaning it. When he was finished he rolled the pack up again, and when he left the tent he saw a plume of red dust approaching from the unpaved road ahead. Nine began honking once he saw Four. He pulled up, grinning, his face red with sun and dirt.

"Hey, you bastard! Did I miss dinner?"

Four said nothing.

"You ate nutrition bars and water without me? And don't tell me I missed the *crackers*!" Nine said, laughing. He got off the quad and did a quick jog in place, as if to free himself from the cramps in his legs. "I'm kidding. But listen, I saw a place up ahead that we can both get to, a real place to eat. Very clean food. Very safe. And I found a couple of boys who can come and watch our stuff while we're gone. I thought of everything."

"No," Four said. "Now sit down."

Nine's smile faded. "Excuse me?"

"Sit down. I'm the primary here, so I insist you sit down. I'm your superior."

"You're the primary? You're my superior?" Nine stared into Four's eyes. "Those are fascinating statements."

Four's stomach tightened. He had not expected Nine to challenge his authority. This was, after all, Nine's first assignment and Four's sixty-third. Though the company didn't assign hierarchy in their two-man crew, seniority should have been implicit and beyond debate.

"I need to talk to you about the job you're doing," Four said evenly.

Nine smiled again. "Listen, let's go get some food and talk about it there. The second we get there, two boys will run back here and will guard the vehicles. I met them last night. These are good boys. I met their parents. Their moms run the food place where we're going. Deal?"

"I'm not going anywhere," Four said. "I've already eaten, and I'm staying with the vehicle because my contract requires me to. I don't want local food, and you shouldn't either. You're acting like a child on holiday. I was in that cab for nine hours today and saw you twice."

Four watched as Nine seemed to take this in, opening his mouth as if to respond but finally deciding against it. He walked away for a few steps, then returned, shaking his head in a show of theatrical contrition.

"Actually, I'm sorry," Nine said. "You're right. You do have a difficult job, and you've been doing it well. I'm grateful, and the people I've been meeting—they're incredibly grateful, too. You should hear them talk! Earlier today a mother came to me carrying her kid, this boy who had some kind of terrible infection in his leg. It looked like elephantiasis. She said the moment the road's finished, she can take him north to the capital and get it looked at. I met a shopkeeper who said that using the previous road system, during the rainy season, he had nothing to sell and his customers had nothing to buy. There was no way to get stuff this far south. But our highway eliminates all that. He'll be able to get resupplied every week, every day even. You know what he said? 'This is like being born again.' You have no idea the isolation they've faced. Most of them have never seen a real doctor."

"That's all fine," Four said. "But—"

"Listen," Nine interrupted, "we don't have to go eat together. But I want you to experience what I did last night. So I'll watch the RS-80. You take the quad. Just go straight about a couple kilometers ahead and you'll see a path heading west. Take that through the stand of trees and you'll see a clearing, and that's where the village is."

"No," Four said.

"You can meet the old man I met. He'll be wearing a white hat with a wide brim, something like a fedora, and he'll shake your hand and tell you thanks. He'll feed you well. Oh, and he has these daughters, so coquettish—"

"No. No!" Four roared. He had been steadily losing his patience. Nine's neck snapped back, shocked by Four's volume. Then he smiled, briefly, as if amused by this new display of emotion. "Fascinating," he said.

Four looked into the forest behind Nine. He knew to pause now, before he said something regrettable. His wife had admonished him years ago about this, about thinking a solution could come through quick, blunt force.

"I didn't mean to raise my voice," Four said. "But the schedule is paramount in my mind. The government is paying for this road, and they have planned a parade. You're aware of this?" Nine's face was blank. "It's set for the twentieth of this month," Four continued. "We can't miss this date. Hundreds of thousands of people are counting on this schedule. If you care about the people here, you'll do everything you can to make sure we make the date."

Nine took this in, and Four thought he saw a man becoming enlightened in real time. He seemed to finally square his actions with how they might affect the people he claimed to take so much pride in helping.

"I get it," he said. "I do. We'll make the date. I promise." He squinted down the road, in the direction of the village he'd intended to take them to. "But you know what hospitality's like in a place like this. I really should at least tell them we're not coming. Otherwise they'll be waiting all night for us."

VIII

NINE DID NOT return that night. Four watched him
drive up the road in the rust-colored dusk, ostensibly
to cancel the dinner arrangement. Four crawled into his
tent, installed his earphones and eventually fell asleep.
Some hours later he woke to urinate, and when he stood
on the roadside, a sliver of moon up and bright, he saw no
sign of Nine or the quad. It was half past three. When he
woke again at dawn, he unzipped his tent and found the
quad parked neatly on the shoulder, and Nine packing up
his tent.

"My superior awakens!" Nine said.

Four ducked back into his tent without answering.
Over many years Four had nurtured the ability to mute
all feeling about such a person or problem. He had been
frustrated by Nine for almost three days, but now, knowing he could not change him or control him or convince

him to be effective in any way, and knowing that Nine was not, in fact, impeding the work on the road—he was merely a distraction—Four could set Nine and his behavior aside. He could place him in a glass box behind which he could not be heard.

"You want to know what happened last night?" Nine asked.

Four decided he did want to know, if only because it would be helpful to the report he planned to write about Nine at the end of the job.

"You missed some good food. It was lamb. I hope you know what a big deal that is, to have lamb in a place like this right after a war. It must have been the only god-damned sheep for a hundred miles. Anyway, they really know what they're doing with lamb. Have you had lamb in this part of the world?"

Four rolled up his sleeping bag and tied it tight. He pulled the poles from his tent and it collapsed like a doused flame. Nine did not move to help, but followed Four around the roadside as he got ready for the day.

"So I got more information about the parade. You know about the president and his wife?"

Four said nothing. Four dropped his tent in its sack and walked up the embankment to pack it into the exterior storage compartment of the RS-80. When he turned around, he almost bumped into Nine, who had followed him to the vehicle. Four began circling the machine, checking it for any irregularities. Nine trailed inches behind him.

"Apparently she was killed in a car accident during the war. She was the president's first wife but he had some others, too, or some kind of arrangement with some other consorts, or what do you call them? Concubines? Concubines. Anyway this was his first wife, and they'd known each other since they were kids. He loved her and she was some kind of altruist, and during the war would visit victims of the fighting on both sides. I mean, the people who told me this last night were on the rebel side but even they had such respect for her, it was really moving.

"Then she was in this car accident which no one thinks was an accident. She was visiting injured soldiers—child soldiers, I should say—in a hospital run by some NGO. And she left the hospital and was driving to the airstrip when her truck got sideswiped by a person-nel carrier. This huge truck crushed her truck like an accordion. They never found the driver of the other truck, but it had some rebel materials inside. You hear about this?"

Four had read something about the incident in the

company's preparatory materials but it held no particular interest. Who killed whom in a conflict like this was not his business, and whatever he might read in a primer was likely so far from the truth that it scarcely warranted his close attention.

"That's what makes this whole truce and the parade such a hopeful thing," Nine continued. "I mean, this president—they assumed he was just consumed by rage and revenge over his wife's death or murder or whatever it was, but he submitted to the international . . . to the whole peace process, and the fighting ended. And the parade was his idea. He built the road, and planned this parade, in what I have to say was a pretty monumental and selfless gesture of reconciliation. Even down here among the former rebels, they see him as some kind of—well, not a saint, but as a statesman. Someone who has the vision and appetite for forgiveness that you need after such a heinous war. I think that's why he got them to disarm so dramatically. I mean, the rebels gave up everything, more than I think they had to. Now it's supposedly one big combined army, but shit, can you imagine? When ever has that worked out so well? Anyway, this was mostly told to me by this one woman. Wait, remember I mentioned the girl from the other night? The chaste story I was about to tell you? She danced a certain way?"

Four recalled Nine talking about such a woman, and acting out her way of moving. "No," he said.

"Well, for some reason she wasn't there last night. But there were so many others, and one of them was talking my ear off about this. We were all sitting around a fire they had going in a kind of sawed-off oil drum. And all around the fire there are these shining eyes, and they're all looking at me while this one girl's telling me the whole story about the president's wife, but meanwhile I felt like a little bunny surrounded by wolves. These were all women, mind you, and they're all drinking rice wine. There was a hunger in their eyes that just bores into you. I felt objectified, I have to say." Nine manufactured a lascivious chuckle.

"I guess it's my hair," Nine continued. "They're always touching it." He ran his dirty fingers through the ends of his greasy hair. "They kept saying things about movie stars, how none of the men here wear their hair like this."

Four stepped into the cab and started the engine. He scanned the diagnostics and made sure the first pod was warming. He had about ten minutes before the asphalt would be ready. He stared ahead at the unpaved road, thinking he could close the door to the vehicle and at least dull Nine's incessant blather.

"So after dinner, there's *so* much that happened," Nine continued. "Everyone brings stuff to me. I don't know what they're giving me, what they're just showing me. One older guy wants to show me a picture of some aid worker he knew twenty years ago. So I go to his house and we look at that, and he gives me some of his own homemade hooch. It's putrid but fucking strong. It tasted like a rancid orange."

Four counted the minutes till the RS-80 would be ready. About seven and a half.

"So in about twenty minutes we'd drunk all this booze and were playing dominoes but honestly I couldn't see what the hell we were doing. It was too dark and my eyes weren't working so well anymore. And I swear the guy's cheating. It's just him and me playing dominoes, no money on the line, and the guy is cheating. I mean, what would be the point? Pretty soon I wake up and I have my head on this guy's little table, this little iron side table with a grating on top. I wake up and I've got a crosshatch on my face, right? And the guy laughs and laughs at me. He's laughing so hard I actually wondered if I was in some kind of hell. And still I can barely see anything. I thought that hooch would make me blind, right? So we go back to the fire and now there aren't as many people. Some of the girls are gone now, maybe taken home by their parents. But honestly, before I could get to the rest of the people at the fire, this hand comes out and grabs me."

Four felt the sudden grip of Nine's fingers. To illustrate his story, he'd reached up into the cab to take Four's arm.

"Don't do that," Four said.

"That's how strong this girl was. She yanked me away from the fire and she basically dragged me into the dark and toward the woods, and all the while I'm trying to see which one of the girls from the fire she is. I don't even know, right? I can only see the side of her, the back of her, just vague shapes as she's walking, with just a bit of moonlight. We go about two hundred meters from the center of town and she leads me into this building, which must have been a school. There was a chalkboard on one wall, and white paper strewn on the floor. Otherwise it was burned out—no roof, no glass in the windowframes, just a dirt floor. The dirt floor is important, because once we're inside she points to the ground, where she's got

63

some kind of mattress or padding there in the corner. She wants me to lie down in basically a crackhead's bed. This is where she wants us to get it on."

Two minutes more, Four thought.

"So I sit down, but I'm not planning on taking off my clothes. She sits next to me, and then sort of leans against me like we're on a picnic looking at a river or something. I start stroking her hair and she starts murmuring, and it's like a cat purring but way too loud, you know what I mean? It just seems too loud on a quiet night in a village with no other sounds around—and we're not all that far from the homes. So I stop stroking her hair and she sits up again and looks me in the eyes. Her face was about an inch from mine, so close that her two eyes looked like one. And that's when I realized that her breath was fucking disgusting." Nine laughed uproariously. He laughed a deep and genuine laugh that caused in Four a brief surge of rage.

"I don't know if *she* knew that," Nine continued. "And I was thinking, *Fuck me, I can't kiss this mouth.* And that's when she just hops on top of me, straddling me like I'm a tree and she's planning to shimmy her way up to the top. I mean, I couldn't breathe for a second, she was holding so tight. She had me inside her in seconds. I had assumed she was a virgin but there was no way. She knew where to find me and where to put me, and I have to say, she played me like a harp. I mean, she strummed every string, she made a symphony of me. I'm *still* vibrating."

The RS-80 was ready. Four closed the door, put it in gear and began moving. Nine, his eyes wounded and surprised, stepped away from the machine and watched it pass.

The day's work was steady and, just as with the day before, Four decided to press on through lunch, eating in the RS-80 cab. Nine had gone up ahead and Four hadn't seen him in an hour. After being momentarily distracted by the black charred carcass of a jeep, Four turned back to the road to find a small boy standing directly in his path, twenty meters ahead.

Four hit the RS-80's alert, a spiraling sound, more like an ambulance siren than a traditional vehicle horn. He expected the boy to leap aside, as most people would in the face of an enormous yellow machine. But this boy did not move. He was no more than four feet tall, and Four guessed him to be about eight years old. He was barefoot and naked but for a ragged shirt and gray underwear, once white.

Four thought about stopping, but knew that pausing the RS-80 here could cause a number of issues—including a rib in the asphalt that was impossible to avoid even with the new machine's improvements. The paver was built to slowly taper off the asphalt release, and sudden stops caused imperfections. So he continued. He sounded the siren again and turned on the lights. But still the boy did not move. The sensors indicated he was seven meters away, which meant he had less than ten seconds to convince the boy to leave the path.

Four opened the cockpit door and waved to the boy. "Move!" he yelled, and swung his arm wildly. The boy turned to him, and for a moment Four was relieved. There seemed to be a certain new recognition in the boy's eyes, as if startled from a reverie. Four ducked back into the cab, but when he looked at the road again, the boy still had not moved.

Four increased the volume of the siren and set the lights to a rhythmic flashing. But the boy stayed in place.

Four slowed and stopped the paver, set the engine to idle, and the screen began to count down from forty-five, after which Four would have to begin moving again or deal with a full reset.

As the vehicle stood still and hummed, Four jumped down from the cab. He walked toward the boy, sweeping his arms in the direction of the forest on the side of the road. But the boy, who had turned his attention to Four, would not stir.

Four had no choice but to do what he knew the company strictly prohibited him from doing. He had to move the boy. As Four moved toward him, he did not expect the boy to react in any way, but the boy surprised him by raising up his arms and allowing himself to be lifted.

The boy weighed nothing at all. From a distance he had seemed exceptionally thin, like most of the children of the region, but that did not prepare Four for the strange feeling of holding a human being who seemed hollow. He had the heft of a marionette. Four, conscious of the time he had left, perhaps twenty seconds, hurried the boy to the side of the road, set him firmly there, and rushed back into the cab.

When he sat down, he saw the counter at three seconds. He'd made it in time, and recommenced forward movement. When he looked up, he feared and half expected that the boy would be there again, standing in his previous spot in the center of the road. But he was not. He had not moved from the new spot where Four had placed him. And as the machine moved past him, Four felt tremendous relief that the boy was safe, that the machine needed no resetting, and he would keep his schedule. As he passed the boy, Four waved, stupidly hoping to confirm that whatever they had just done was now finished, but the boy did not wave back. He only stood, looking with the same curious intensity as before.

The last hour of the day was without further anomalies. But he did not see Nine. When Four had reached the next day's first pod, he powered down the RS-80. He took the tent out of the storage compartment, found a suitable spot on the road and assembled it. He unrolled his sleeping bag and placed his knife and gun inside. He left the tent and looked down the road for sign of Nine, and saw none. It was still an hour till sunset.

Four returned to the tent and lay down his head, thinking he might nap before dinner. But when he closed his eyes, he could only think of the boy. A strange feeling came over him, a nagging sense that there was something wrong with the child, or wrong with the child's circumstances. Four had a sense, in fact, that the boy was still standing where he had left him. And all at once it occurred to Four that the boy had been lost. He had expected Four to help him reunite with his family. Instead, Four had simply carried him to the side of the road and continued on.

Four reminded himself it was not within his mandate to carry boys at all, let alone reunite them with their parents. And yet it was only five o'clock, and Four had at least ninety minutes of light. He had already interacted with the boy once, so doing so again would not involve any greater risk. He could leave for a few minutes and keep the RS-80 in sight.

He dissassembled his tent, locked it into the vehicle and walked back in the direction of the boy. The asphalt underfoot was still warm, the oatmeal smell faint but everywhere around him. As he made his way up the incline he inspected his work, finding it flawless. It was the first inspection of the road he'd performed since he'd begun this job—the inspection was supposed to be done by the secondary, on the quad—but Four found it enormously useful to see the road now, to see how the bitumen was settling and cooling. As he walked, Four reminded himself that the company encouraged regular physical activity. He was accomplishing two of his directives—inspection and exercise—while walking briskly back toward the boy, a distance he guessed to be about two kilometers.

Soon he saw the boy. He was no longer standing but was sitting on the side of the road, not far from where Four had left him. The boy watched Four approach but did not move. He only watched Four with his intelligent eyes until Four, who was out of breath and who had soaked his jumpsuit with sweat, was upon him.

"Where do you live?" Four asked.

The boy made no attempt to answer. He couldn't understand Four's language. Four made a series of gestures—a mother, a father, a home, a bed, food, the act of eating. The boy paid attention, and seemed in every way alert and even willing to understand. But he said nothing and did not stand up and seemed almost incapable of movement.

Four checked his watch. It was 5:40. He had just under one hour to help this boy and to get back to the RS-80 and set up his tent again before dark. He had no flashlight with him.

"This way?" he asked the boy, pointing into the forest lining one side of the road. The boy nodded.

"Okay," Four said, and scanned the dense trees. He planned to carry the boy through the forest and to his home, with the boy guiding the way. He lifted the boy, astonished again by the boy's weightlessness, and walked down the embankment to where the trees began.

"Through here?" Four asked, pointing.

The boy nodded again.

"Good," Four said, now feeling more confident. It seemed only a matter of time before this was resolved. The boy had heard the machine, had wandered away from home to see it, had gotten lost, and now Four was bringing him back to his family. The schedule was not compromised, and this action might even reflect positively on the company.

When they were through the first few trees, though, Four saw another of the ominous signs, the skull and crossbones rendered yellow on black. The forest was mined. Four stopped in midstride, one foot in the air. He scanned down, looking for a trigger. The ground was covered in needles and leaves. If there was a mine here, he would not see it.

It was madness to thread his way through a mined forest while carrying a child. He decided to return the way he came, and knew he would have to mind every step, landing each one precisely where he had before. Seven steps. He turned and stepped slowly on the outside edges of his feet, trying to place as little of his weight on the ground as possible, expecting at any moment to hear the click of a mine being activated, to feel the obliterating shrapnel and fire.

Another step, and another. The boy was preternaturally calm, his hand gently resting on Four's shoulder. Four stopped to breathe, and could smell the boy's salty skin and dusty hair. He adjusted the boy in his arms, moving him from one side to the other, careful not to change the weight of his body, and then made the final few steps out into the light.

Four knew he had no recourse but to return the boy to the spot where he found him. Perhaps his parents expect him there, he thought. Perhaps they saw him walk to the road and would be looking for him there. So Four conveyed the boy awkwardly, his arm serving as a sort of throne for the child. He carried him back to the road and up the embankment. He placed the boy's tiny feet, light as a newborn deer's, on the new asphalt, and stepped back. The boy looked around, as if orienting himself, and then he looked to Four, as if knowing Four would be leaving. He made no complaint.

Freed from the boy's weight, Four doubled over and gagged. He knelt, his breath short. He stood and paced and punched his thighs. The closeness to death, to his death and the boy's, affected him more than he expected or desired. *Harness,* he demanded of himself. *Harness this,* he thought. *Harness, harness.* He turned one last time to the boy, waved and strode back to the RS-80.

He retrieved his tent and set it up, ate two nutrition bars and a bag of nuts and waited for Nine, mulling what he would say to him when he arrived. He pictured himself yelling but decided on an even, urgent tone punctuated with caustic words.

When he was finished assembling his tent and had arranged his bedding, he stepped out into the cooling night air and only then did he notice that he'd set up his tent in the shadow of an enormous boulder. He couldn't understand how he'd missed it earlier. There were no other such rocks anywhere near this, a landscape that so far had been flat and uninterrupted by any outcropping—hundreds of miles from even a foothill. The boulder clearly had not moved in millennia, but it had a tilted disposition that implied it could begin rolling at any moment, crushing Four first.

He wanted to move his tent but he knew it was irrational to do so. He could not give in to superstition or weak-minded fears, so he left the tent where it stood. Inside, he unrolled his pack, inspected his knife and pistol and placed them under his pillow and in his sleeping bag. All the while he cursed Nine. It was Nine's responsibility to deal with anomalies like the boy on the road. Nine spoke the language, and would have been far more adept at knowing whence the boy came and what he needed. But Nine was nowhere to be found, and had left it to Four, which risked the schedule, and risked the boy's life and Four's.

Beyond his irresponsibility and shirking of all duty, Nine had been leaving Four alone at night, which was expressly against company protocol and any rational notion of security. There was at least some chance that the interaction with the child had come to the attention of the locals, who might be angered by it. This was a primary reason for the company's policy of nonengagement with local populations. All words, gestures and actions could be misinterpreted and lead to delays, debates or, worse, to reprisals and violence. Four was seldom frightened, but now he conjured the image of a group of men arriving, angry about his handling of the boy. They could be genuinely enraged or they could use it as pretext for a shakedown. If men were to come, they would come that night, he was certain. He was so close to where he'd encountered and carried the boy that Four could easily be found. If Nine were here, they would have some degree of safety in numbers. But Nine was not here.

Impossible to work with, Four would write in his report. He had resolved that a report made after this assignment would be necessary. He would not alert the company to any of the present difficulties, but after the fact, when he was home, he would elucidate it all. *Lacking all maturity and seriousness.* He would be sure that Nine never worked for the company again. *Incapable of maintaining attention to the work at hand.* Four installed his headphones and pressed play.

IX

AT FIRST LIGHT, Four woke to an unnatural quiet and realized he hadn't heard Nine return the night before. He rose, left the tent and saw no sign of him. The quad was gone.

Normally this would be alarming but Four knew it likely meant nothing. Nine was not in danger; he had simply stayed elsewhere. Standing outside the tent, Four poured a protein packet into a cup of water, stirred and drank. As he was finishing, he saw a burst of dust come from a rocky slope ahead. Nine descended the hill and joined the road, riding the quad recklessly and still wearing the purple scarf. His helmet was gone.

"Did I miss breakfast?" he asked.

Four could muster nothing to say.

"Sorry I wasn't back last night," Nine said. "I was up ahead, around that corner actually, yesterday afternoon,

75

when I came across the most incredible thing. There was a group of men and even some women trying to move the husk of an old airplane. I think it was from the 1950s. Do you know anything about planes?"

Four turned to begin disassembling his tent. He couldn't look at Nine.

"This looked like an old bomber," Nine continued. "It must have been shot down during the war. It was on this precarious outcropping, and the whole village was trying to move it down to flat ground. They planned to use it for a shelter. The thing was big enough to sleep thirty. So I was cruising by and saw what was happening, and volunteered to help. I had no choice, right?"

Four packed his tent into the RS-80's storage compartment and locked it.

"So we tied the quad to the fuselage and about twenty guys pushed, and I gunned the quad, and pretty soon it started moving. It was incredible! We dragged the thing a hundred meters to the middle of town. Now it's like the centerpiece of the village. The kids were playing in it, and we found a parachute, so the women started cutting that up for clothes and blankets. Fucking extraordinary."

Four was counting the number of infractions Nine had committed already and lost count at ten. Engaging with the local population. Misappropriating company property. Using a quad, which the company had flown five thousand miles, to haul a fallen bomber? If anything had happened to the quad, Nine would have had to walk to the capital. And his helmet was gone. This man was a vortex—all rationality was devoured within him.

"And then of course they had to have a big party to celebrate the whole deal. There was fresh meat. They never tell you what kind of meat. And more wine. I know it's technically illegal but everywhere you go they have wine. This was different than the wine from the other night. But incredibly strong. And I was offered someone's daughter again! But she was too young. Maybe fifteen. Beautiful and tall, and they insisted she was a virgin, but I couldn't do it. Was I wrong? I felt bad, so I gave her father my helmet. I gave them everything I could."

Four unlocked the door to the cab. Nine was still talking.

"Man, that was tempting. I mean, why not? She'd be getting married any day now anyway, right? I'd definitely be a better husband than some old man, right? After the war, all the younger men around here are dead."

X

AGAIN FOUR ATE his lunch without stopping. He had
not seen Nine all morning and had had no impediments.
The day had been steady and meditative, the roadside
unpopulated and bare. As he finished the last drops of
his bottled water he saw on the screen that the road was
approaching the only bridge on the route to the capital.
He squinted into the distance, and soon could make out
the faint outline of a steel bridge traversing what looked
to be a forty-meter river span. A different division of
the company had designed and built this bridge, Four
knew, so he had no qualms about crossing it with a
thirty-four-ton machine. In other countries, on other
assignments, he had crossed locally made bridges and
overpasses and did so with great trepidation. There was
only so much engineering expertise in the world.

As he drew closer, the bright glimmer of the river's

slowly moving water emerged. The depth was no more than four feet at its center, with rocky embankments on either side, where women squatted, using aluminum washboards to scrub their clothes clean. As the RS-80 met the bridge's beginning, Four could see a group of boys wading in the river's shallows. They were splashing, kicking, the droplets of riverwater shimmering and falling like fireworks.

Four thought of typhoid. This was an area of high risk and he didn't want to think of the probability that one of those children would contract something from playing in water like this, carelessly splashing it into one another's mouths. If infected, what recourse would any of them have? There were no doctors from here to the capital.

One of the boys, taller than the others, began waving in the direction of the bridge. Four looked closer and saw that it was not a boy but a man who was waving. A lean man with long hair. It was Nine. Nine was frolicking in the water with the local boys. Four looked up and down the river, and saw the quad on the opposite bank, parked precariously on a steep incline. Nine continued to wave, as if needing confirmation from Four that he had been seen.

The RS-80 was making its way across the bridge and Four needed to concentrate, but his mind was upended by this new outrage. Every other offense committed by Nine was somehow within the range of behaviors with adult precedent. But this, jumping in the river in the middle of a workday—a river that carried with it towering risk of infection—sent him spiraling. Now Four could dismiss him. This was a fireable offense and it proved the operation was better without him than with him. The dismissal would be brief and there could be no argument. He would allow Nine to drive the quad back to the point of origin. The company would fly him home, wherever that was. He didn't care and didn't want to know.

Four had crossed the bridge by now, and did not expect to see Nine again for some time. But a few minutes later, Nine flew by on the quad, head down, and in some seeming effort to appear professional, he was wearing his jumpsuit again and had discarded the purple scarf. He continued up the unpaved road until he was out of sight. Four smiled to see him disappear.

It was late afternoon when Four saw the first blue tarp. Amid the high scrub it emerged, looking like an oversize kite stuck in a thicket. As he got closer he saw more blue tarps, all of them being used as roofing for makeshift homes and shops in a medium-sized village. The rains were coming, Four remembered. As he approached the belly of the town, people began to walk across the road in front of him, as if the highway were already finished and he was just another motorist.

The market was alive with people and music. Silver corkscrew plumes rose from small fires. Scooters and motorcycles buzzed across the road and into the thick of the market. Four could not stop the RS-80 but could see there were countless businesses operating near the road already. His work was almost superfluous, it seemed; the unpaved road had already created this town.

One man, who was better dressed than the others, waved and motioned Four to stop. Four shrugged to convey that he could not stop, so the man walked alongside the vehicle, and motioned Four to roll down his window. Four shrugged again, indicating the window did not open. The man walked alongside patiently, and every time he caught Four's eye, he again made a rolling-down motion. Four stared ahead, ignoring him.

Finally the man walked so close to the RS-80 that Four could see his large long-lashed eyes and his handsome but weathered face. Four took him to be about fifty. "Hello!" the man yelled, projecting his voice through the glass. "As you can see, the road is very popular already!"

As the man walked, a large silver medallion danced around his sternum, hanging from a black leather strand.

Four said nothing. The man continued walking alongside the vehicle, keeping pace with Four's window. Four had the sensation that the man had nothing in particular to say—that he only wanted to practice Four's language and to show the other locals that he could converse with the man making the road.

"Do you need any assistance in your work?" the man asked. He gave his name but Four didn't register it. He did not want to know this man's name. Such men frequently offered to do odd jobs, to clear the road, to bring water, to keep people from the embankment, any number of tasks that were wholly unnecessary. Sometimes these men were genuine workers looking for an honest day's pay. Sometimes they were hustlers looking for an angle, a bribe. Four knew that, outside microenterprise, there was virtually no source of income in the region, that it was an area of subsistence farming and sporadic employment through the nascent government.

Four shook his head and looked ahead, pretending that the paving of the road required his full attention. The man took this news in stride and continued to walk alongside the paver. They were now past the main part of the town and the roadside structures were less frequent.

"You will be finished in how many days?" the man asked.

Four looked at his screen, ignoring the man.

"How many days until you are done with the road?" the man asked.

Four said nothing.

"Excuse me," the man said, showing no sign of fatigue or annoyance. "The road, how long until it is completed? Don't worry. I am not one of yesterday's rebels looking for work."

Four held up eight fingers.

"Excellent," the man said, walking briskly and squinting into the distance. "With a road like this, now it is possible to make plans."

Four waved curtly, hoping he might convey an end to the interaction. Instead, the man moved closer, tapping on the window and pointing down. Four did not react.

"I heard about your concern for the boy," the man said. He mentioned this without any inflection or apparent knowledge of how strange it would sound to Four.

"He is the son of my cousin," the man said. "He was interested in your machine and wanted to watch it. He said you lifted him and carried him into the woods. Then back to the road."

Four was not sure what to say. He could not plausibly

deny that he had done this. He wondered if he had violated some local law or custom. It could prompt some contrived interaction with local elders or authorities.

Four stared ahead. The next day's first pod was only fifty meters away and the sky was darkening with cloud-cover. When he reached it, he had no choice but to stop. Avoiding the man would be impossible.

Now he could see that there were two teenage boys standing on top of the pod, waving to Four, as if the pod had been missing and they had located it for him. He rolled down his window and waved his arm, motioning them to get off. They did nothing. Finally the man stepped purposefully toward them, his medallion swinging wildly as he roared at them in a guttural tone utterly different than the gentlemanly one he'd been using with Four. The boys quickly jumped down and scattered.

Four nodded to the man, being careful not to thank him. Thanking him would imply that the man had performed some task worthy of compensation.

When Four reached the pod he stopped and shut down the RS-80 and, hoping to avoid the man with the dancing medallion, he stayed in the cab, pretending to check his gauges. He ducked low, almost hiding beneath the dash. When he sat upright again, the man was standing by the cab door, his hands at his hips, looking back at the road already paved.

Four opened the door and stepped down.

"Very nice work so far," the man said. "It's black like licorice. I have never seen such a road."

"Thank you," Four said.

The company insisted on ignoring locals but recommended against being rude. That could create its own complications. The balance to be struck was formidable.

"Very nice work so far," the man said again.

Four retrieved his pack from the exterior compartment on the vehicle and spotted a location just down from the embankment where he could assemble his tent. All the while, the man followed him.

"You will be safe here," the man said. "Tomorrow it will not be as safe. That land up ahead is more contested." The man pointed up the road with a long tanned finger. Four was perplexed by his age. His face did not look more than fifty, and his gait was as light as a boy's, but his hands looked like the gnarled ends of a petrified tree.

Four extricated the tent from its container, and the man watched with great interest as the tent, with a shake and a tilt, created itself. Four hoped that ignoring the man might expedite his departure, but the man showed no signs of leaving. Because he had been walking with the vehicle, and had been seen talking to Four, and because he had cleared the teenagers from the pod, in the eyes of the villagers, a few of whom were watching from a distance, the man appeared to be a kind of partner now to Four.

"I greet you," the man said. "The people here would like to honor you with an event. It will be a very good event, with our best food. A calf will be sacrificed to celebrate your road. It will be one of my own animals, the best of what I own."

It was strictly against company policy to be feted in this way, especially in a region like this, one divided by tribal animosities. Spending time with any one tribe in an asymmetrical conflict such as this could be seen as choosing a faction, and nothing was more hazardous.

"No thank you," Four said firmly. He realized that by speaking to the man, he was crossing a line. The last few projects Four had completed had required no speech whatsoever.

"I'm afraid the arrangements have already begun," the man said. "It would be considered impolite not to accept."

Four was unconvinced. He had heard this canard before. "I didn't ask for a party. I can't leave this vehicle."

The man looked perplexed. He squinted into the white sky. "My people will watch the machine. No harm will come to it," he said. Four said nothing. The man persisted. "We must be able to express our hospitality. It is part of our culture. Our pride will be damaged."

Four suppressed a scoff. To be pressured into hospitality was no hospitality at all. "No. No. I can't," he said. "I have nothing to say about the pride of your people. I'm passing through. I'm doing my work. I want to be ignored and forgotten here. That's all. Thank you," he said. He ducked into his tent and considered zipping the door closed, but that seemed too aggressive. He lay down, put his earphones in and pressed play. He could see the man's feet through the tent door, and eventually he saw them move away. When he was sure the man had left, he sat up and peeked his head through. The man was still there.

"Where is your other man?" the man asked.

Four had found this to be the rule: even in areas without phones, and with virtually no electronic communication network, there was always intimate knowledge of the road's crews and their progress. This man knew about the boy and he knew about Nine. It could be presumed he knew more, too.

"He's making sure there are no problems," Four said. He pointed to the unpaved road ahead.

"You will soon see where much fighting happened," the man said, looking toward the lilac horizon. "It was where the first rebel attack on government soldiers occurred. Many battles after that took place there. A region of constant atrocity. Creative atrocity. There are still rebel fragments there."

The man played with his medallion for a moment, and then returned to the subject of Nine.

"But your man isn't up there. When I last saw him, he was on a back road, traveling that way," the man said, pointing at the paved road behind them.

XI

FOUR WENT TO bed early, in part to end his engagement with the man with the medallion, who hovered around his tent for an hour before leaving. Four woke at just after two to a rooster's mad wailings. He unzipped his tent to relieve his bladder and found Nine still gone. There was no tent and no quad.

The night was quiet and soaked in black. There was no electrical grid in the region, so the nights were unsullied by human striving. Four looked up to a moonless sky, only a shard of starry space visible through the cloudcover. The rooster screamed again and Four returned to his tent to finish his sleep.

He awoke with the dawn's bloodless light and again found no sign of Nine. He ate a breakfast of compressed nuts and dried fruit and packed his tent into the RS-80. He planned to get most of a standard day's work done by noon, and then allow for the vehicle to cool before embarking on a second, extended session in the afternoon. Nine's absence was emboldening. Without him, Four could complete a day and a half's work in one.

Throughout the early morning he was relieved to see no sign of the man with the medallion. By 8:00 a.m., Four had paved five kilometers without incident. The foliage that had until then served as an emerald colonnade gave way and the land opened up into a kind of wide flat plain, devoid of trees and dotted by mounds of rusted steel—dead machines. Some were recognizable as burned jeeps and pickups. There was a downed and half-charred helicopter, its rotors limp. This was the contested area Medallion had mentioned. A pair of stray dogs were chewing at a carrion bird. High above, vultures circled, waiting for their turn. Brick buildings in the distance bore the white star-scars of artillery fire. The structures had all been rendered roofless, the jagged walls now reaching fruitlessly to the sky. Amid the destruction there was a group of young men playing volleyball. They briefly stopped to watch the RS-80 pass, then resumed. At the edge of the town, before the trees again overtook the landscape, Four saw a large black heap, gleaming in the sun. When he got closer he saw that it was a high hill of plastic garbage bags, the same sort he'd been seeing since

he left the southern city. Until now he'd seen the bags
alone or in groups of one or two. This small mountain
of the full and jagged bags indicated a different level of
organization and intent. It reminded him of the mountains of tires in rural parts of his own country. He did not
know what became of mountains like this here, though,
and could not imagine what kind of machine might
eventually address a hill like this. Perhaps, he thought,
this was to be the country's dump.

A loud rapping startled him. Someone had struck the
window of the cab. He turned to find a woman, elderly
but fierce. She wore a night-blue wrap and her hair was
uncovered and wild. She was walking alongside the paver,
tapping his window with a long staff of polished teak. He
looked ahead, waiting for her to tire and recede. But she
only tapped louder.

He turned to her and shooed her away. She tapped
again, and now pointed to the mountain of garbage
bags. Four assumed she thought he could take care of
it somehow—that the man paving the road could also
pick up a mountain of trash. Did she mistake him for
someone involved in waste management? He shrugged,
and then pointed to the road ahead of him. He pretended
to concentrate on the work again, but she walked in front
of the RS-80 and waved her arms above her, trying to

stop the vehicle. He flashed the machine's headlights and waved her away. He was determined not to stop. A few feet before the paver overtook her, she stepped out of the way and strode quickly to the other side of the cab. She waved her hand wildly in front of his window and again pointed at the garbage mountain.

"What do you want me to do?" he said inside the cab. He threw his hands up for her to see. He had no role in any of that, he told her, and eventually she stopped and returned to the woods.

By noon Four had finished twenty kilometers, the most he'd paved in a morning, and he stopped in front of a new pod to eat and let the paver cool. There was no sign of Nine. He had spent the last few hours furious with Nine, who should have prevented the encounter with the old woman—an encounter that was highly dangerous for her and for the work at hand. Had she slipped and caught a limb under the machine, the project would be finished and the schedule unmet. He needed to do something about Nine. Something harsh, something punitive. There were no precedents for this.

Four retrieved two nutrition bars and stepped out of the RS-80. Standing on the cooling asphalt, he ate them quickly, stuffing their wrappers in the pocket of his jumpsuit. A buzzing sound wove itself into the fabric of the sky and he looked up to see an airplane approaching high above. It seemed to be following the path of the road, and when it flew overhead he saw that it was an old bomber, probably from the 1960s—one of the many secondhand planes the government had used to bomb villages in the south. Now, in peacetime, he assumed the government was keeping tabs on the road's progress. Four was satisfied that they would see that he was on or ahead of schedule.

Chewing on a vitamin C pill, Four pictured Nine in some kind of trial. Perhaps he could be prosecuted for financial damage done to the company. Perhaps he had committed crimes back home. It was not unusual for criminals to pursue work like this—far away, far from the pursuit of police or victims. Four found these visions of Nine being tried satisfying, like a good hard itch.

In the distance Four could see a small settlement of stone and thatched dwellings, some buttressed with sheets of corrugated aluminum. The shrieks of children spiraled over the roofs and he saw the caterwauling forms of two boys dart from one end of the village to the other, red dust rising in their wake. Closer to him there was a dull thump and the sound of water splashing. He turned to see a young woman bent at the waist, freeing herself from a long pole that she'd been carrying across her back to balance four jerricans full of water.

She stood and stretched her arms upward, yawning and turning her torso, and then, after these seconds of respite, she crouched again under the long pole and arranged it across her shoulders. Slowly she lifted the jerricans, but halfway to her standing, one of the jerricans, resting in a notch on the pole, began to slip, and Four found himself running toward her. The pole tilted wildly. Two jerricans slid and splashed on the ground. Four ran to her to help, and in those few seconds he saw her terrified eyes, saw her cower, saw her move away from him, saw her ready to abandon her possessions and run.

He stopped short of her and raised his hands. She stepped farther away. He tried to explain his intentions. She did not speak his language. Fool, he called himself. Something about the elderly woman had twisted his mind, allowing him to do things he knew never to do.

Now that he was close, he saw that she was far younger than he'd thought; she looked no more than thirteen. She had a long face and close-set eyes, small teeth and bright gums. She looked desperately around her, her eyes on the village in the near distance. She seemed ready to scream.

"No, no," Four said, and backed away. He continued to retreat, his hands high above his head—he didn't know why he was doing this—and he backed away until he reached the vehicle. He climbed inside quickly, started the engine and activated the next pod. He looked straight ahead, giving the girl time to escape unseen. When he finally turned around again she was halfway to the village, her four jerricans well balanced though she was running.

Four decided he would call headquarters. This latest encounter was Nine's fault, he decided. Every deviation found its origin in Nine's neglect. Had Nine been nearby, the woman would not have gotten so close. Four wouldn't have been in this position, in terms of schedule or location. He wanted to do violence to Nine, and this call would be a kind of violence. Nine would be dismissed for this. The company would tell Four to keep the schedule, that they would send someone from the capital, most likely via helicopter, to retrieve Nine. Again Four pictured him at trial. There would be no trial, could be no trial, but the image presented itself to Four and gave him satisfaction. Nine's head hung low, repentant.

The company, though, would also ask Four how it came to be that Nine had deviated from protocol. Where had Four been during all this? they would ask. And how had Four, as Nine's superior, allowed all this indiscipline? Four would protest, would explain that Nine had left despite his admonitions, that he could not control the man. But this would not suffice. Four's good record would be tarnished. Four was known for work without complication. A good worker does not report problems; he fixes problems. Four decided against calling the company. Silence was clarity. Silence was power.

He retrieved a bottle of water and drank deeply, and as he did he realized there was a possibility that Nine had been kidnapped. If so, this would mean the kidnappers would find Four, and would ransom him, too. There was also the possibility that Nine had simply been robbed and killed by bandits. Certainly in a place like this the quad was worth enough to take one man's life.

Without evidence, Four grew more certain that Nine was dead, and decided that he would now work at a doubled pace, to finish the work as soon as possible, and he would sleep in the RS-80. Seeing the battlefield earlier in the day had jarred him more than he had realized.

He looked ahead at the dirt road, russet red and dry as chalk, and then looked behind him, at the black highway. A shape appeared as he stood squinting into the distance. It looked to be a motorcycle and was moving quickly. He could make out a man on it, but could not make out the man's face. The insect buzz of a small diesel engine broke the quiet.

Four thought of retrieving his gun from the vehicle. He had time. But he hesitated long enough that soon it was too late; the movement would be too sudden and provocative. So he stayed where he was and raised an arm in greeting. The man on the motorcycle did not reciprocate. Four thought again about diving for his gun. But finally the man lifted his chin and the sun illuminated his face. It was Medallion. He waved his gray-palmed hand to Four as he swung the bike to a stop.

"Yes!" he yelled. "Yes! I found him. There is trouble. He sent me." Medallion was out of breath as he stepped off the bike. He held his hand over his chest to slow his heart. "I found him in the tent. Very ill. He said he cannot move. I told me I was a messenger from you. He told me that he will stay there until he feels better. He said it was no problem."

"How far back is this?" Four asked.

"Twenty kilometers, twenty-five," Medallion said.

"And he's alone?"

"He is with my cousin. My cousin stayed with him and lent me his bike."

"He can't move?"

"No. He has no shirt on, and just he lays there on his back. His eyes are closed. He has a high fever. I gave him some water and put food by his bed."

"What sort of food?"

"Some bread, some biscuits. I think he will be fine. It looked like some minor poisoning to me."

"Poisoning?" Four asked. "You mean food poisoning?"

"Yes, yes," Medallion said, and pointed an ancient finger into his mouth.

Four knew that the best thing would be to have Nine brought to him. As if reading Four's thoughts, Medallion said, "I asked him to ride back with me but he said no, he cannot lift his head. He said to leave him alone."

"He has to be brought here," Four said.

"Yes, I know this," Medallion said.

"Do you have more cousins nearby?" Four asked. "Maybe the one who lent you this bike?"

"Yes, many cousins," Medallion said.

Four asked Medallion if he could ride with a cousin on the motorcycle, the two of them, to Nine. They should, he said, bring with them some sort of plank with which they could fashion a gurney. Nine would be attached to the gurney, and this gurney would be attached to the quad. Carrying Nine, Medallion would ride the quad back to Four.

While Four was speaking, a confused expression had come over Medallion's face. Finally he asked, "What is the quad?"

Four explained the nature of a quad, that it had four wheels and was built for off-road usage. He tried other words for it—ATV, small car, large motorcycle.

"Ah, yes, I know this vehicle," Medallion said. "But there is no vehicle with the man."

"Are you sure?"

A new, grim expression came over Medallion's face. "I think it is stolen. This is possible."

"Did he tell you this?" Four asked.

"No, I didn't know about this vehicle before you just mentioned it. So I did not ask about it. Maybe he doesn't know?"

Four thought for a moment. The quad could be stolen. But a suspicion bloomed inside him, that this was all a ruse and that Medallion had something to do with it. Four tried to work out the play happening here, the next few steps. There would no doubt be ransom for Nine, ransom for the quad.

"Excuse me," Medallion said, "I know he said he can

stay there alone, but I do not think this is good. It is not common for a foreigner to be harmed here, but the robbing of the vehicle is a problem. It makes me think. The road brings new people to the area, and their behavior might be different from ours."

Medallion played with his necklace.

"I think I should bring him to you," he said. "It is not a problem. There are many ways to carry him."

XII

FOUR STARTED THE RS-80 and shut the door. He cursed himself for not trusting his instincts sooner. He should have fired Nine on day one. Nine had broken crucial covenants that first morning and yet Four allowed him to continue. It was appalling, all of it—Nine's behavior and Four's inaction.

The cab vibrated alive and Four's anger dissipated. The ideal would involve Medallion bringing Nine to the last pod of the day. They could install Nine in his tent and Four would try to diagnose him, treat him with some of the medicines he had in the RS-80. He had antibiotics, antimalarials; Nine would be better in a day. Four would call headquarters and someone would retrieve Nine, most likely by helicopter. No matter Nine's health, Four wanted him gone.

Then a pale memory of nighttime sounds came to

him. Some recollection of clicking at night. Of someone in the vehicle. He had been deep in dreaming and had not woken, but the premonition now grew louder, more insistent. He shut down the RS-80.

Four opened the compartment that held the first-aid kit. The compartment was empty. His adrenaline spiked. He opened every compartment, to no avail. The kit was not in the vehicle. Someone had removed it. Four's gut insisted it was not Medallion. Medallion was not an actor, was not capable of this long ruse. Four knew it was Nine. There could be no doubt. Nine had found some reason to take the first-aid kit to one of his villages. He had given it away.

When he was seized by fury, Four made plans. He planned to call the company. He planned to insist they remove Nine immediately. Now there were two reasons to do so: he was ill and he was a thief. He would be removed, and then Four would file a report. It was a criminal act to appropriate the first-aid kit, depriving both of them of critical self-care in a land virtually without medical expertise. It was a grievous crime and he would seek all available legal remedies against Nine. Four had never wished ill against another human, but he wanted grave consequences visited upon this man.

Four threw open the compartments again, planning to make the call to headquarters, even while knowing he should not do so. Not yet. He knew he should not call anyone in this state, that the remedy for Nine's crimes should be administered with cold execution. But he was in that unique fugue state of knowing he was acting rashly but so deeply savoring its delicious vengeance that he could not hold back.

He searched but could not find the satellite phone. He found a toolkit—held in a similar hardcase—and opened it, knowing the phone would not be within. He worked in an unthinking rage, opening every compartment four times and finding no phone. He tossed the guns and knives and cash aside. He emptied the compartments of the flares and flashlights. And with a growing dread he realized the phone was gone, too. Nine had taken the phone and had given it away.

Four calmed himself and slowed his breathing. Now he thought briefly of murder. By stealing the first-aid kit and phone, he had greatly endangered Four's life. He had brought him far closer to death than he'd been with these protections; it was like driving Four to the edge of a cliff. It was tantamount to murder, so Four's contemplating actual homicide was not irrational. It was logical. It was next.

He had to work. He had to be contained and moving, so he started the machine and worked through the afternoon, calmed by the straightness of the road as it passed, undeviating, through grasslands and briefly under a canopy of tortured oaks. Under dappled white light Four noticed a vehicle to his right, driving on the embankment. It was Medallion, hunched over in the cab of a tiny three-wheeled vehicle, a tuk-tuk with a small truckbed. Another man rode a motorcycle in parallel, his face stern with purpose. Medallion pointed to the truckbed behind him, and sped up so Four could see a figure there, covered in a tarpaulin. It was Nine. His limbs were stiff and his face was gray, his tightly closed eyes facing the sun. His pallor and rigid posture were those of a dead man. So Nine was dead. Four's stomach knotted, and he realized he did not want Nine dead, that Nine dead would be far worse than Nine inefficient or meandering. Finally Nine's mouth opened like a drowning man's gasping for breath. He was alive. Four felt only faint relief.

Four paused the RS-80 long enough to instruct Medallion to bring Nine to the road's next pod. Medallion readily agreed, and it wasn't until Four had restarted the paver that he wondered why Medallion was doing all this. At some point, certainly, he would demand compensation. Being in Medallion's debt greatly increased the chances of further, and possibly worse, complications. Entering into any financial transaction in a postconflict zone like this was perilous. No deals were fixed; all was malleable. And once funds had changed hands, word would get around that Nine had cash, and there would be no end to the trouble.

Four paved eleven kilometers in the last hours of the day, uninterrupted and alone, until he was within sight of the final pod. One of the sensors indicated that the RS-80's paint supply was running low, and Four turned around to make sure the double yellow line was still covering steadily. He saw a pair of vehicles moving quickly toward him, and his first thought was of a bouquet of dying roses. There were six or seven men in each truck, each of them wearing a red beret. Four hadn't seen any men in uniform since he'd left the southern city and immediately assumed he figured into their intentions. The trucks were coming up the road at great speed and the men were clearly armed. He did not panic. He knew the probabilities and he knew his options.

He let the RS-80 continue to run. Stopping would be a mistake, a concession, an admission. He slunk down in his seat, so as not to alert them that he was retrieving a weapon. He opened the box under the seat and found the handgun and put it under his left thigh. He fumbled for a grenade and put it under his right thigh, and all the while the trucks grew louder until they seemed to be directly behind him.

He looked in the rearview mirror and found they were only fifty meters away but had slowed. He took them to be a breakaway rebel group. They planned to ransom him, Four assumed. Or, to defy the president, they planned to take Four and to capture or destroy the paver. From his sunken position in his seat Four continued to watch as they drew closer. Between the two trucks there were twelve men, but now that he could see their faces they seemed strangely casual. A few were talking, laughing. Only the driver was looking forward.

Four was just another assignment, another kidnapping, he assumed. He reconsidered his gun and grenade. He would surely die if he attempted to use either. He tried to put the grenade back in the box under the seat but couldn't make it fit. He opened one of the compartments in the dash and dropped it inside and then took the gun and slid it into his jumpsuit. He would be frisked and they would find the gun but would not begrudge him for having armed himself. Now he waited.

He considered where they would keep him while

they sought a ransom from his company. He would first try to buy them off himself and if that didn't work he would tell them whom he worked for and how to reach them. The process could be over in days, he knew, but could last months. Workers had been held for years. He glanced into the mirror again, knowing that by now they must be upon his vehicle and ready to force him to stop, but instead he watched as the first truck turned down the embankment and onto a dirt path running perpendicular to the highway. The second truck followed, and he saw the second truckbed, also full of men with red berets, descend the embankment and disappear into the woods. A minute later, a military helicopter emerged from the tree line and banked hard, following them.

Four reached the final pod in the early evening. For the hour after the trucks had almost overtaken him, he had been disarranged—his body calm but his head churning. He could not form linear thoughts. His visions of their plans and his imminent detention were so florid that the reality, wherein he was unharmed and simply sitting in the cab of the RS-80 and continuing his slow work on the road, was far less plausible. He expected the rebels to return. He expected to be thrown from the cab and tied up. But instead he had come upon the final pod, powered down and stepped out of the cab under his own power. Just ahead he saw Nine's tent assembled at the edge of the trees. A man was standing by the tent, the man who had been in the truck cab with Medallion. He nodded to Four and pointed to the tent. Its flap was open and Four could see Nine's prone legs, Medallion kneeling beside him. The smell of feces seized the air. Someone had shat in the tent, he was sure. Four's mind fought itself. He wanted to know how sick Nine was and what the remedy might be. He wanted to know if Nine had stolen the first-aid kit and phone and given them away. He wanted to know if Nine knew anything about the disappearance of the quad. But he also had no desire to see Nine, fearing his own fury.

Medallion emerged from the tent.

"He is very ill," Medallion said.

"Typhoid," Four said.

"Or malaria. Or a bacterial infection. Or something else. You and I are not doctors."

Four suppressed a volcanic rage. Nine had gotten sick on his own accord and had eliminated all options to help him.

"The ride here was not good for him," Medallion continued. "He had a bowel movement on the way and then again when we stop here. His stomach is very swollen."

Medallion's friend was at the tuk-tuk, wiping down the truckbed with a rag. The presence of Nine, and the animal power of the man's offal, brought Four into the moment again.

"There is a clinic not far from here," Medallion said. "It is a foreign woman who runs it, she speaks your language. I think the man needs her attention. He needs antibiotics. We can go, and my cousin will watch the vehicle."

"But we had antibiotics," Four said. "Did he tell you this? Did you see any medicine? Maybe he gave it to you?"

Medallion looked very confused. "No, no. He had this medicine? Where was it? You still have it?"

"No," Four said, and now he knew that Medallion could be trusted. He spoke directly. He looked Four in the eyes. His reactions were genuine. He knew nothing, Four was sure, about the quad or the medicine. Everything Nine had lost he'd lost on his own. Four explained that there had been medicine in the vehicle, but that Nine had likely given it away.

"Then we go to the clinic," Medallion said, his long fingers holding his square chin.

The news that there was a clinic close by gave Four great strength. At the clinic there would be doctors, perhaps someone from his own part of the world. He would be able to talk all this through. He could get information about whoever the rebel group was. He could stay there for a day perhaps. Perhaps he could even leave Nine with the clinic. Yes, he thought. Nine was sick and he could leave him with the medical professionals who could not ethically turn him away.

"I saw two trucks," Four said. "They were full of armed men in uniform. They weren't any uniforms I knew."

"Actually I know these men," Medallion said. "These are just opportunists. Bandits posing as politicians. You acquire two trucks and some business cards and you have a rebel movement. They are not to be worried about."

"They got very close to me," Four said.

"And they left you unharmed," Medallion said.

Leaving the RS-80 unattended by company staff was strictly prohibited, so Four proposed that Medallion take Nine in the tuk-tuk.

"There is no road from here to the clinic," Medallion said. "It is only a narrow dirt path. The tuk-tuk will not make it. But we can take the motorcycle. You will go with me and we will get the doctor and bring the doctor back. Your friend should not be moved again, I don't think. My cousin will stay with him and the machine."

Four realized that technically he would not be leaving the RS-80 unattended. Nine, a member of the company staff, was remaining with it. Again he cursed Nine and the situation he'd created. He could not let him die, which would ultimately reflect on Four. He had no choice but to seek help, but to do so he would be riding into the wilderness with a stranger and would be leaving the RS-80, an invaluable machine, and would be leaving Nine, too. If Four was wrong about Medallion, it would take no time at all for Medallion and his companion to dispose of both Four and Nine and do whatever they saw fit with the paver and all within it—its weapons and cash.

"How far is it?" Four asked.

"Not far," Medallion said. He was already on the motorcycle.

Four strode to the tent and ducked inside. Again he was assaulted by the smell, its feral violence. He held his breath and saw that Nine looked very much like a corpse, with his hands at his side, his palms open and pale. His face was oily and inexpressive. Four crawled into the tent, his nose in his shirt, and put his finger under Nine's nostrils. He felt the faintest of exhalations. Nine's powerlessness, the way he had pulled the efforts of all these men toward his rescue, brought a new fire to Four's lungs.

"Did you give our medicine away?" he asked.

Nine made no indication he could hear or respond.

"If you stole it, you committed a crime. And you might have sealed your own fate. You could die. Do you understand? Do you understand the consequences of your actions?"

Nine's eyes remained closed. Four left the tent.

"This is my cousin," Medallion said, and Four shook the hand of Medallion's cousin. Cousin bore little resemblance to Medallion. Where Medallion was tall and thin, with high cheekbones and feline eyes, Cousin was shorter, rounder, with a slablike face and small round eyes tucked into his flesh like the buttons of a pillow. He said nothing to Four.

"He doesn't speak much of your language," Medallion explained. "But he will watch over the man and the vehicle. He was a soldier in the war. He is very capable."

Medallion started the motorcycle and inched up on the seat, making room for Four. Four swung his leg over the seat, and Medallion sped into the woods, winding through low trees on a path that Four could not discern.

The land was uneven and dry, and the ride very rough.

Medallion routinely had to slow and walk the bike around a tight turn or down a sudden slide. Four's arms and legs routinely scraped against the brittle branches of the low scrub. Thirty minutes had passed when Four asked if they were getting close.

"Not far," Medallion said.

It was another hour, the sun having set and night coming quickly, when they saw, up ahead, a broken mosaic of light visible through the woods. Medallion turned to Four, making sure he'd seen it.

"The clinic."

When they came upon it, Four saw that the building was no bigger than a trailer, but by the standards of the region it was lavish. The building was new, the grounds well kept. A satellite dish stood on the roof.

They approached the compound, their feet crunching on a path of small polished stones. Inside, two people were watching soccer on a large screen. Medallion knocked on the door, producing a tinny sound. Neither figure inside moved. Medallion knocked again.

"Come back in an hour," a woman's voice said. "Barça's on." And then she let out a low, breathy laugh. Four peered through the door and saw a blond-headed figure sitting on the couch facing the television. He could not see her face. On the overstuffed chair next to her, a man's dark-haired head sat in profile, looking both at her and the game, as if unsure if she truly planned to ignore the visitors.

"Excuse me?" Medallion said.

"We're closed!" she said.

Four assumed she was joking, that she would get up now and come to the door. But the woman stayed where she was and resumed watching the television. Medallion turned to Four, as if to confirm they should proceed. Four nodded.

"Excuse me, ma'am," Medallion said. "We have a sick person here."

"How sick?" she asked, but still did not get up. The other person in the room said nothing. Again he looked to the door and back to the blond woman before returning his rattled attention to the game.

"We don't know, miss," Medallion said. "He has not moved for two days."

"Food poisoning, probably," she said.

"I fear it's worse," Medallion said. "The symptoms are like typhoid."

Finally she turned to see who was speaking to her. She glanced at Four, then leveled her gaze at Medallion. "He looks okay to me."

"This is not the sick person," Medallion said.

The woman had turned back to the television. "Where is he, then?" she asked.

"About ten kilometers west," Medallion said.

"Our truck's broken," she said.

"I can take you to him," Medallion said.

"Who is he?" she asked.

"He is a worker for the new road. This is the other worker," Medallion said, nodding to Four. "They are building the highway to the capital."

Four assumed this information would motivate the woman to quicker movement, but it had the opposite effect.

"Well, we're not here to treat visiting construction workers. Our mandate is indigenous women's reproductive education and the health of newborns and children." She took a tall plastic container of water that had been sitting on the table in front of her and drank from it.

"But I have seen you in the villages helping others," Medallion said. "You gave medicine to my male cousin."

Now the woman stood and came to the screen door. She was no more than thirty, with a smooth oval face and small eyes, a blond bob gripping tight to her skull like a helmet. Her T-shirt recommended eating a certain kind of kale. She remained on the other side of the screen, her face gray behind the tight aluminum grid.

"That was incidental," she said. "I have no authorization to treat the tummy aches of foreign contractors. And it's likely not medicable. And I can't travel ten kilometers to do it."

Now the other aid worker came to the door and stood behind her. He was tall and was dressed like a missionary, in black pants and a white dress shirt.

"Missus," Medallion said. "Actually it is not necessary for you to travel to the patient. If you give us antibiotics we will administer them ourselves. We both have experience in this."

Now a sly smile overtook the woman's mouth. "This is starting to sound fishy," she said. "Conveniently, the patient doesn't come with you. You don't want me to see him, but you want *me* to give *you* drugs. And you'll administer them *yourself*?" Her eyes were alight with mirth. "Who are you planning to sell them to, just out of curiosity? Oh, and tell me the price you're getting. I should probably know what the market will bear."

Medallion looked at the ground and spoke in an indignant rumble. "Missus. We are not selling the drugs."

Four decided it was time for him to step in. "Doctor," he said, though he guessed she was not a doctor.

"I'm not a doctor," she said. "And how did you get past the guard?"

"The guard recognized the urgency of this situation," Medallion said.

"Nurse—" Four began.

"I'm not a nurse," she said.

"Please!" Medallion barked. His eyes were wide with rage. Four reached over to calm him, holding Medallion's forearm with his fingertips. The physician's assistant had crossed her arms in front of her, a show of defiance, but her jaw trembled.

"Okay," Four said, calmly, "we are part of a major construction concern in the region—"

"So fly in your own doctor," she said.

"We can do that next time. But for now—"

"But for now you thought you'd shake down the local clinic first? What is the name of your company?" She said this as though she intended to issue an official complaint to Four's CEO.

Now Four was finished with niceties. "Miss. You're being bizarrely unreasonable. We're in a region devoid of doctors or medicine. But you have medicine. A man is very ill not far from here. Your Hippocratic oath, I believe, compels you to help this man. You stand in dereliction of every ethical norm."

The woman was no longer smiling. "If you come back here again, I'll report you to the local police, the authorities in the capital *and* the UN. You'll be swimming in inquiries for years, and I know how unhappy your corporate overlords will be with that kind of scrutiny."

She closed the screen door and then a second, opaque door within. She pulled the shades on the window, and all light from the building was extinguished but for the green glow of the television.

XIII

MEDALLION DROVE SLOWER on the way back, and soon Four realized that he was running out of gas. The motorcycle sputtered into a hacking cough and expired.

"I'm sorry," Medallion said. "I thought we would make it."

Four asked how far they had to go, and Medallion guessed it would be an hour's walk. They took turns pushing the bike on the path that without the motorcycle's headlight was nearly invisible. Medallion trudged steadily forward, occasionally looking up at the sky's cloudcover, as if hoping for a break that would reveal the stars or moon and provide some orientation.

"I'm very sorry," Medallion said again. "Watch your step."

The path dipped where it crossed the cracked expanse of a seasonal stream.

"No, no. You've been a great help. I want you to know that I appreciate it," Four said.

"I am selfish in my help," Medallion said. "I want this road finished myself. My wife has been ill, did I tell you this? She has a problem in the liver. The capital is the only place that can help her. She needs maybe a transplant. Before the road, it would be four days' drive in a crowded bus to the hospital in the city. She could not do this. Now, though, when the road is done I can take her in my tuk-tuk. Do you smoke?"

Four said he did not. Medallion laughed.

"I thought maybe I could borrow a cigarette from you. I think your friend might have cigarettes, no?"

"I don't know," Four said. "I don't think so."

"Ah, look," Medallion said, and pointed to the moon emerging from the clouds. With the landscape now illuminated Medallion adjusted their course slightly, and continued pushing the motorcycle.

"Actually the boy is fine," Medallion said. "The one you carried. But he has something wrong with his mind. During the war there were so many medical issues for the babies. The midwives and nurses went north for jobs, so the babies here were born without help, and problems happened. So many mysterious sicknesses."

"Yesterday I tried to help a woman who was carrying water," Four said. "She got scared and ran away."

"Yes, she would probably not want this. Actually it is not acceptable for a man like you to talk to a woman alone this way. There were so many ugly things that happen during the fighting. The men, they take the women many times. They just take them."

"They raped them?"

"Yes, they rape them."

Medallion smiled at Four, as if apologizing for these rapes, for having to inform Four about them.

"Most of the young women go hiding. But if they are found, they are raped. Sometimes it is for enjoyment of the soldiers. Sometimes it is for punishment of some man. They rape the wife or sister or daughter."

Four didn't want to talk about this anymore. But his silence implied to Medallion that he should elaborate.

"So the woman you met with the water, she is worried about what you will do. She doesn't want to be raped by you. It is likely she was raped before. Sometimes it is a neighbor who rapes. He has always desired the woman and sees the war as a way to have her. Actually my wife was raped by a neighbor this way. And then the neighbor was killed. I'm sorry the woman with the water did not accept your help."

"It's okay. It doesn't matter. I'm sorry for your wife."

"They could hide here," Medallion said loudly, sweeping his hand across the rough terrain, thick with foliage and outcroppings. "It helped many of us in the war. Men and children, too. We became millions hiding. There are so few roads, such narrow paths. The government army could not get to us, could not find us. But now we are ready to move into this century. There is still some old hatred between us and them, but the road, I think, will be the end of that. The road brings understanding, I think. Have you been to this country before?"

Four said he had not.

"When the work is done, will you return?" Medallion asked. "You have a home with my wife and me."

Four had never returned to the site of any job he'd completed. "No," he said. "I won't be back."

"Yes, yes." Medallion laughed. "God loves an honest man. Watch your feet."

A large plastic bag lay in their path. Four had almost stepped on it. It was the same kind of black bag he had seen all over the countryside. "What's inside these bags?" Four asked. "I've seen them everywhere."

"The waste of war," Medallion said dismissively. "But I have a related question for you."

"Okay."

"It is delicate, I think."

Medallion walked in silence for a few moments, his face pained, as if trying to find the words.

"What I would like to ask," he said, finally, "is do you think you could help me with a university degree?"

Four was flummoxed. "Help you get a degree? I'm not sure what you mean."

"I have heard about ways to get a degree from universities through correspondence," Medallion said. "I have to stay here, but perhaps I can study at one of your universities this way, with letters in the mail. Do you understand? Is this a possibility?"

Four told him that when he returned home he would try to send Medallion whatever information he could.

"Very good, very good," Medallion said.

"But I have to ask you," Four said, "how is that question related to the bags of waste I asked about?"

"Without the war and its waste," Medallion explained, "you would not be here."

XIV

WHEN THEY RETURNED to the RS-80, there was an amber glow inside Nine's tent and the silhouette of a sitting man. Four had the momentary impression that Nine had recovered, but when he entered, Four found Cousin kneeling above Nine, his palm on his chest. He spoke quickly to Medallion.

"He is checking his heart," Medallion said. "He was a medic for part of the war."

Though Four was dubious about Cousin's ability to assess Four's heart with such a method, he found himself waiting for a diagnosis. Playing his part, Cousin listened for a moment and then nodded. "Bad," Cousin said.

"You speak my language," Four noted, surprised.

"Some," Cousin said.

"We received no help from the clinic," Medallion told him.

"Go back tomorrow," Cousin said firmly. "She change her mind."

"No. She'll only grow more determined not to help us," Four said. "She'll only grow more stubborn and aggressive."

Cousin spoke quickly to Medallion, and Medallion seemed to agree. "He says we can find local medicine," Medallion said. "There are some good people. Perhaps fifteen kilometers from here. Near the marshes."

They all knelt around Nine.

"We go tonight and come back tomorrow," Medallion said, and crawled out of the tent. Four followed. Medallion and Cousin siphoned a few liters of gasoline from the tuk-tuk and transferred it into the motorcycle's tank. Four did not want to be alone with Nine. His condition was likely to deteriorate. He had no kit, no tools, no expertise. But he could not express these fears to the two men helping. Medallion started up the motor-cycle and Cousin got on behind him.

"You keep the tuk-tuk here," Medallion said, and gave Four the key to the vehicle. "If the man needs help you follow the road back to us. I think you know the road, yes?" He smiled.

Four watched Medallion and Cousin speed away. He returned to the tent and fought the smell and sat cross-legged above Nine, startled by the extraordinary trust Medallion had just demonstrated. He had left the tuk-tuk. He was spending a night on the road to find a medicine man.

Four had attributed to Medallion so many nefarious motives and plans, but now Medallion had shown himself to be the better man. In any place in the world there were criminals, there were schemers and cowards. And everywhere there were men like Medallion, ignited by purpose. The burden of his wrongful suspicions, the weight of his shallow judgments, brought Four to a state of exhaustion, and though he had planned to set up his own tent, he found himself unable to muster the strength. He lay down with his head at Nine's feet and let sleep take him.

XV

IN THE MORNING, Nine's condition was unchanged. Four sat above him, checking his breath, which was still shallow. He leaned down, smelling Four for signs of jaundice or kidney failure, and found his odor normal enough for a sick man who had not bathed in days.

The high-pitched whine of a motorcycle overtook the air. Four left the tent and waited on the road until he saw Cousin speeding toward him. When the motorcycle drew closer, Four could see that there was another man with him. It was not Medallion.

Cousin parked the bike and shook Four's hand. The second man, far older than Cousin, was wearing a long robe and a fedora. He carried a modern nylon backpack.

"Medicine," Cousin said, indicating the older man, though the man did not pause for Four. He strode directly to the tent and crawled inside.

"My cousin home," Cousin said. "Wife sick."

Four and Cousin followed the medicine man into the tent, where they found him kneeling near Nine's ashen head. After examining Nine and talking for a time with Cousin, the man uncapped a small plastic bottle he'd brought, full of milky liquid, and tried to bring it to Nine's mouth. Nine was too weak to lift his head. The doctor dipped the bottle into a cloth and brought it to Nine's lips.

The medicine man was exquisitely patient. Passing an ounce of the liquid into Nine's mouth took half an hour. There was some faint indication that Nine's body was accepting the fluid and was wanting more. The man continued for a spell, and was able to get a few more tablespoons past Nine's lips.

Finally Nine closed his mouth and turned away. The medicine man spoke for a time to Cousin without looking at Four. His tone was indignant, as if he had been brought to the patient too late to be of use. He gestured at Nine and then Four, showing his lower teeth, all of them crooked and irate. After he was done speaking, Cousin turned to Four with sympathetic eyes, as if apologizing for the man's strident tone.

"Man very sick," Cousin said. "We go. My cousin come again." Quickly Cousin and the medicine man got onto their motorcycle and, before Four could argue, the two men were gone.

Four was alone with Nine, whom he now understood to be a dying man. After sitting with him for a time in the tent, its walls aglow with the rising sun, he felt an unfamiliar strain on his eyes. His throat grew dry. He had not cried since he was a boy and would not cry now. But the helplessness overtook him. He could not leave Nine, but if he stayed, and Nine died here, what then? He would bury him by the road and continue, yes, but then Four would be fired, fined, shamed. How does one man let another man die while paving a road? The company would suffer grave damage to its reputation in the region and around the world. The deadline would be missed and the parade would be lost.

Four left the tent and stood on the road. A rooster wailed. A small airplane flew low and crossed the sky, trailing a neat white line that bled messily into the cloudless blue sky. Four decided that he would not leave Nine and would not begin working on the road again until a plan with Nine was in place. He could spare one day. And he believed that Medallion would return.

Four sat on the side of the black highway, his legs extended down the sloping shoulder. He installed his earphones and in the warming sun he grew calmer and more resigned. He could not do much to save Nine. If he was sick, it was entirely his own doing. Hundreds of thousands had died during this country's civil war and the world had scarcely taken interest. Now some adventuring imbecile had acquired an elective sickness and was paying its price.

Four thought again about burying Nine. It would have to be near the road, he decided. Or would it be more honorable, and more in keeping with Nine's embrace of the local people, to allow Medallion to dispose of him in some traditional manner? Four didn't know what the local custom was. He hadn't seen a graveyard that he could remember. Maybe they would burn him. There was no correct answer, Four thought, and anyway it hardly mattered. He would be dead, and no one Nine ever knew back home would come to a place like this to visit his burned or buried and decomposing flesh.

A dark object appeared, coming from the south, the heat of the road blurring its shape. When it drew closer Four could see it was a vehicle speeding toward him. He climbed into the cab of the RS-80 and waited, watching through the rearview camera. He expected the approaching vehicle to be another rebel truck, but as it approached he realized it was a blue sedan bearing small rebel flags. Its driver unknown behind tinted glass, it slowed as it came upon the paver, and finally stopped ten meters behind. The rear passenger door opened and a tall man in military dress emerged.

Four had retrieved his handgun and installed it within his jumpsuit. He chose to wait inside the vehicle. It underlined that he was a professional, an extension of the machine.

The military man's face appeared below his window. He was a broad man of about forty wearing what appeared to be a mismatched uniform. His pants were green and his shirt and jacket were gray, his beret the same dull red Four had seen worn by the men on the jeep. There were three stars on his shoulders, and Four took him to be a general. His catlike eyes were large and wide set and stared at Four impassively until Four rolled down the window.

"I assume you are on schedule," the man said. His voice was low and hoarse, as if he'd spent the previous night screaming. He scanned the road ahead, squinting into the distance as a pair of mirrored sunglasses, the lenses perfectly round and spotless, hung from the top buttonhole of his uniform.

"I am," Four said.

"I assume you have not been bothered?" Now the general looked behind them, as if he might catch a glimpse of any past incidents that might have impeded the paving.

Four knew not to mention any encounters. Nothing good could come from involving a rebel commander in this work.

"Not at all," Four said.

"Excellent," the general said. "It was my job to make sure the roadbed was clear and without local interference. I am gratified that your work has proceeded without delay. The timing of the parade is crucial, as you know."

"We'll make the schedule," Four said.

"You are alone. You have a partner, yes?"

"He is scouting ahead," Four said. It was a small lie laden with small risk if the military man heard or saw evidence to the contrary.

"If you have any issues, you contact me," the general said, and produced a business card with worn, rounded edges. He returned to his car, and his driver swerved around the RS-80 and sped up the unfinished roadway toward the capital.

It had not been two hours since Cousin and the medicine man had gone before Four again heard the high buzz of the motorcycle. This time, though, it was Medallion, and Four felt a great smile overtake his face. Medallion smiled, too, though his eyes and furrowed brow betrayed his confusion.

"Is the patient feeling better?" Medallion asked. He made his way toward the tent, and Four could tell he had misunderstood Four's happiness.

"No, I don't think so," Four said. "I was just glad you came back."

Medallion had changed his clothes and was now wearing a bright yellow dress shirt. He stopped at the tent door. "The medicine man told me your friend is so sick. It was too late for him to help, he said. I think we need antibiotics or stronger medicine from the woman at the clinic." Medallion looked into the distance, his long fingers touching the sharp corners of his chin. He turned back to Four with a grim smile. "So I have been thinking of an idea. But it is not one you will approve of."

"Please tell me," Four said.

"The nurse might not want to give you the medicine, but there are other ways to get it."

"Cousin?" Four asked, guessing that Cousin, an ex-soldier, might have some way to break into the clinic.

"Cousin? No. No," Medallion said. "My cousin will not steal. But there are other men." Medallion seemed to be weighing it in his mind, then exhaled quickly as a decision arrived to him. "I think it is the right thing," he said. "It is the only way."

Medallion left on the motorcycle to find his men, and Four was again alone with Nine. It was midday and the heat was stifling. Four had propped the tent's door open and yet the air inside was humid with human decay.

"Medallion went to get medicine," Four told Nine. Nine did not respond. Four did not bother saying anything else. All day Nine existed in a state of catatonia, his breathing weak and eyes half open. Four had not seen a man die, but Nine looked much like photos he had seen of men on their deathbeds, eyes retreating into the skull like independent creatures giving up before the larger battle was lost. His lips were chapped and lined with a ghostly purple fringe.

Four could see no outcome but the death of this man, in this tent, and likely that day. But Medallion had been hopeful, had he not? When he had left, Medallion seemed optimistic that he could procure the medicine and that it would bring Nine back from his catatonia. Four had lost all bearings. He paced on the newly paved road as the forest's insect hiss grew louder. He was aghast at himself, at what he had allowed to happen. He was counting on the medical assessment of a stranger who was not a doctor. The one medicine man had come and gone and had given Nine to the fates. But Medallion had created a raft of hope and Four found himself climbing onto it.

He thought of the schedule. If they could administer the medicine today, there was a chance Nine could be stabilized in a few days. There was still padding in the time line for Four to stay with him until he recovered. Then Medallion could bring Nine forth at some later date. They could meet in the capital.

In the late afternoon Four heard the high whine of Medallion's motorcycle. He stood on the road and squinted into the distance. Medallion was not alone. There were two motorcycles, each carrying two men. They were coming toward Four, weaving like sparrows, and now Four could see the silhouettes of rifles extending high above their shoulders. Four had the brief and irrational thought that Medallion's kindness all this time had been a deception, that he had been planning from the start to kill and rob him and Nine. As he had the day before, he envisioned diving into the tent to retrieve his pistol. He knew he should; it was only a reasonable precaution. But now that the motorcycles were only twenty meters away, Medallion was waving while Four stood defenseless.

"Good news!" Medallion roared. His eyes were bright, his mouth a toothy adolescent smile. Behind him, his passenger now grinned, too. The men on the other bike, one of whom was carrying the rifle, were less effusive. They all pulled up before Four, and the passengers jumped off. Medallion set the kickstand of his bike, and from his passenger he retrieved two plastic bags and held them over his head.

"We were successful," he said. He crouched down on the road and emptied the bags. There were large bottles of Imodium and ibuprofen, a roll of gauze and packets of plasma and intravenous fluid and a half-dozen syringes. There were bottles of ciprofloxacin and Bactrim, and a vial of amoxicillin. "We got whatever we could take without it being noticed. And look," he said. One of the men gave him a sheaf of papers bound together with tape and with the title TREATING TROPICAL DISEASES. "We have all we need," he said. "A very fruitful adventure."

Four thanked them all, shaking each man's hand, and having no idea what should happen next. He considered asking how it was that they got these things, but thought perhaps they would not want him to know.

"Okay, let us begin," Medallion said.

Ignoring the papers they'd stolen, Medallion crawled into the tent, filled a needle with amoxicillin and injected

136

Nine through his swollen right arm. At the touch of the needle, Nine's eyes clenched almost imperceptibly.

"We will provide him with another shot in six hours," Medallion said. "I think he will continue living."

Medallion's men stayed for dinner. Four provided them with a buffet of his nutrition bars and freeze-dried meals, which the men ate with polite curiosity but without visible approval. Medallion explained that the men preferred not to be known by name, given the theft they had performed, and Four thanked them again for their courage and sacrifice. He knew he would have to compensate them at some point, but trusted that Medallion would work out the particulars.

When they were finishing their meals, Medallion told the story of how they came to acquire the medicine.

"This man here"—and he pointed to the smallest of the collaborators, a wiry man of about twenty-five, with his two front teeth missing from his otherwise handsome face—"his cousin is the guard at the clinic."

This cousin had no keys to the clinic, Medallion explained, but patrolled the compound, watching the front gate. He knew that the blond woman and her two staff members often left the compound to do their work in the nearby communities. So it was just a matter of waiting until they left. When they did, the guard notified Medallion's two other men, one of whom was clever with locks. He was not, in the end, able to open the lock on the front door, but was able to jimmy one of the windows. The third man was the only one who could read the labels in their language, so he climbed through the open window, and found that the locker containing the medicine was held tight with a padlock. Again the lockpicker was called upon. He climbed through the window, too.

"All the while the guard was watching," Medallion said, smiling, "but now he was guarding against the nurse!" When he translated what he'd said to Four, all four men burst into peals of laughter.

"This part was very difficult, and so it was very important to have this man," Medallion said, indicating the lockpicker. He seemed a very serene man, convinced of his competence.

The lock on the medicine closet was a large one, very difficult to pick, Medallion explained, so they knew they would have to use bolt cutters. They cut the lock, and in the locker, Medallion found the appropriate medicines and the booklet explaining the treatment of tropical illnesses. He was careful not to take too much of any one thing, and to take from the back of the closet, leaving the superficial appearance of rows of medicine undisturbed, a closet untouched.

"But how did we make sure they don't know that the closet had been violated?" Medallion asked, raising an eyebrow. More and more, Four was realizing that Medallion was a leader, an entertainer, a man with great charm. "This is where this man is so clever," Medallion said. "He brought with him a number of padlocks, and chose the one that looked most like the one he had cut. Then he attached the lock to the door, locked it and left the key to this lock inside the lock. Our hope is that the nurse and her staff will assume that one of them had simply forgotten to take the key out."

"But what about the other key?" Four asked. "At least one of the clinic's staff has the real key to the original lock, right? The broken one? Won't they try this old key on the new lock, and find that they don't match?"

"Yes, but our new arrangement will confuse them long enough," Medallion said. "And because inside the closet it will look like nothing is missing, they will not be alarmed. Any other thief would take everything from the closet and would provoke much worry."

Four thought about this, agreeing that the entire operation was so strange, subtle and counterintuitive that the nurse and her staff would be flummoxed beyond action.

"And anyway," Medallion said, "that woman will be gone in a month and someone else will take her place, and no one will remember any of this."

After dinner the men stood and got ready to leave. Medallion took Four aside. "These men should be compensated. What is your plan?"

Four had a good deal of local currency in his pack, in the pocket next to his weapons, and he had a second cache inside the RS-80. He pictured himself getting the money and retrieving his pistol at the same time, in the unlikely event the negotiations deteriorated. But he had no idea of the scale for compensation for such a deed.

"How much, do you think?" he asked.

"It is not money these men want. As you know, the local currency is not stable. The men are more interested in your tents," Medallion said. "These are not possible to buy in our country. The way they defy mosquitoes and are so quick to be assembled is very appealing to them. The men say they would like one of the tents."

"But we need these tents," Four said. "There are two of us, and two tents. And Nine is still very ill."

"But two men can fit and be comfortable in one tent," Medallion said. "These men have taken a great risk to get this medicine." He seemed to be speaking now not only for the other men, but expressing his own view.

Four refused, offering half of the local currency he had in his pack. He wasn't sure of its purchasing power, but he had been told it was enough to feed himself and Nine for the duration of their work in the country.

Medallion returned to the men. He spoke to them in a low murmur, and suddenly there was a burst of loud and outraged voices. The men who had seemed so friendly and self-effacing at dinner were now livid and in the violet light took on a menacing cast.

Medallion walked back to Four. "I am afraid this cannot be a negotiation. These men insist this trade is very fair to you. They have done you a great service by saving the life of your friend, and you will not give them a *tent*." Again Medallion seemed to depart from simple translation and looked at Four with his own eyes and gave voice to his own thoughts.

In the silence that followed, Medallion put his hand on Four's shoulder and spoke quietly. "This is the right thing."

And so Four emptied the contents of his tent and put

his things into the one Nine occupied. He folded the tent, stuffed it into its duffel bag and handed it to Medallion, who handed it to the locksmith. All feelings of goodwill were gone.

"Actually there is one more thing," Medallion said then, seeming a bit embarrassed to be amending the arrangement. "These men might be able to find your quad. If they do, they would like to keep it."

"I don't understand," Four said, though as he said the words, he did understand.

"If you have the opportunity," Medallion said, "you don't report it missing. It's gone now, and these men might eventually have it. And when you go back home you can get another. Does that sound fair?"

Four stared into Medallion's eyes. "I don't want any of this anymore," he said.

"Okay," Medallion said. "Then we go."

The men mounted their motorcycles, and Medallion arranged himself on the back of one. "I will return tomorrow," he said, and they sped away.

XVI

IT WAS LIKE sleeping with a corpse. Four felt sure that the medicine would begin working imminently, and had in his mind that the fever would break in the wee hours, but after six hours, and a second shot of antibiotic, Nine showed no signs of improvement. His breath was still broken and he had not moved. Four stared at Nine's back. Four was exhausted and his eyes were heavy, but he felt sure that if he fell asleep, he could awaken to find Nine dead. There would be no struggle, just a quiet expiration.

Four slept fitfully and woke at first light. He checked Nine's breath, finding it unsteady and weak. He crawled from the tent, feeling as if he'd escaped a shared grave.

He stood, stretched and heard the whine of Medallion's motorcycle coming near. But as the motorcycle drew closer, Four saw that it was Cousin, not Medallion.

"How is man?" he asked as he set his kickstand.

"No different," Four said. "Where is your cousin?"

"Wife sick," Cousin said. He ducked into the tent and Four followed. Cousin again put his hand on Nine's chest and listened.

"Bad," Cousin said. He opened Nine's eyelids roughly and turned his face from side to side. "Bad, bad."

Cousin rested his ear on Nine's chest again and listened.

"Bad," Cousin said. "He stay."

"I told Medallion I would have to leave today," Four said. "He said he would stay with Nine until he was able to move."

"Yes," Cousin said, nodding gravely. "I stay."

Outside, the sound of another motorcycle grew louder until it sputtered to an end nearby. "Man come help, get water," Cousin explained.

Sitting in the tent, with Nine prone and rigid beneath them, Four and Cousin discussed the plan concocted by Medallion. Cousin would stay with Nine, and the new man would be able to run for food and water as needed. Medallion would return the next evening and take over. When Nine was able, Medallion and Cousin would transport him via tuk-tuk up the road, to meet Four at the end of the day.

In the last hour, Four had felt a new calm overtake him, an acceptance that Nine would likely die. He had been resigned and panicked before, then hopeful about the prospect of the medicine, but now the medicine was having no effect and he found himself oddly finished with the whole endeavor of trying to save Nine. Going back to work and receiving word of Nine's death or recovery in a few days somehow seemed an acceptable way of proceeding.

"No," Nine said. Four was shocked to hear him speak. He hadn't issued more than a whisper in days. Now Nine's eyes were open. He scanned the tent, seeing Cousin.

"No," Nine said, and his arm rose and he grabbed for Four's face, finding his ear, which he held with surprising force. He pulled down on it. Four lowered his head to Nine's mouth.

"Don't leave me," Nine whispered.

"I have to leave," Four said. "We've spent our extra days. To meet the schedule I have to go. You'll be fine. Cousin is a moral man. Medallion said so. When you recover they'll bring you up to meet me."

Nine's eyes were wild with fear. "I feel like I might die," he whispered. "Something is very wrong with me. My chest feels hollow and cold. My back is numb. I can't feel my legs."

"It's just malaria. You're probably having hallucinations."

"I've had malaria. This is not malaria."

"I can't take you with me," Four said. He knew Nine's words were the ravings of a feverish man, and thought he only needed to finish the conversation, allow Nine to sleep again, and be gone. "You'll be fine. I'll see you tomorrow," Four said, and he believed he would.

Now Nine's hand moved from Four's ear to his mouth. His fingers grabbed at Four's lips and reached into his mouth, his knuckles rapping against Four's teeth. Four pulled away.

"No," Nine said, louder now. "I can't die here alone in a tent. Not with these men I don't know. Please. Please. Think about mercy."

"You're talking. You're stronger now. You'll get stronger."

"No, please," Nine said, his mouth quivering and his eyes suddenly wet. "I ask for your mercy."

XVII

ATTACHING NINE TO the hood of the RS-80 was his own idea. When Four had insisted there was no way to continue the road and transport Nine, too, Nine devised a way.

Four cursed Nine as he followed Nine's directions, using the tent and their blankets to fashion a kind of bed on the vehicle's front hood. Cousin and his friend helped lift Nine, and when they set him down on the vehicle's steel chassis, Nine's hands flailed, grabbing their fingers, discarding them until he found Four's. He squeezed his hand weakly.

"Thank you," he said.

Using bungees and duct tape, Four secured the mound that was Nine. When he was finished, he stood with Cousin and his friend, and they assessed their work.

To avert unwanted curiosity from those Four would be passing along the road, they had been careful to obscure Nine's face. With the tape and bungees crisscrossing the bulbous mass, Four was satisfied it looked like the vehicle was simply carrying supplies on the front hood. In this region, where towering loads would be routinely carried atop tiny motorcycles, a mass like that which held Nine would attract no interest from anyone.

To mitigate the heat from the machine, Four and Cousin had insulated Nine's bed with palm leaves and two layers of waterproof tarp. Four started the vehicle and let it run for twenty minutes, and then checked with Nine. He said he felt no heat beneath him.

"Then we go?" Cousin asked.

"Now we go," Four said.

After an hour he found himself forgetting for long stretches that he was carrying Nine before him like an offering. From his windshield he could not see Nine's face, but they had left an opening in the wrapping through which Nine could raise his arm, gesturing for help if need be.

Cousin and his friend were performing Nine's task of clearing the road, and they were doing so masterfully.

They seemed to be everywhere, circling the RS-80, shooting ahead to investigate and disperse a shepherd and his goats, removing stones, returning seconds later.

For Four, the day became one of unexpected contentment. With Cousin, he was confident the road would be unimpeded. With Nine immobile and held tight to the machine, he could cause no more distraction.

When he reached a new pod, Four had three minutes while the RS-80 set it into place, so he used these periods to check on Nine. The first time, Nine seemed to be in a comfortable sleep. The second time, he was awake and asked for water, which Four was ashamed to have forgotten to provide for sooner. He hastily set up a water bottle near his mouth so Nine could sip at his discretion.

In the late afternoon, Four calculated that he could finish ten more kilometers before it was too dark to see. He would push until seven, two hours later than usual. If he continued at this new pace he could catch up to the original schedule in four days, and arrive at the capital at the date and hour originally promised, in time for the parade.

When Four reached the last pod, he powered down and

went about the laborious process of disassembling Nine's bed and reassembling it inside the tent. Nine refused food, so Four ate alone and lay down next to him. Nine's breathing was rhythmic and loud, so Four put his earphones in, pressed play and spiraled down to a viscous sleep.

XVIII

A LOUD BOOM woke Four. In the murk of sleep he thought it was a cannon, but when he sat up he realized it was the foot of a man kicking the outside of the tent. Voices were all around, yelling and striking the tent with their feet and batons. The sound inside was low and savage. Four saw that Nine's eyes were open and he was very much aware.

"Cousin?" Four said, holding out a vague hope that Cousin was there but had neglected to announce himself. There was another kick to the tent and a booming voice roared through the nylon. Now there were hands on the tent's zipper door. The lock would prevent the zipper from being pulled, but Four knew he could not hope to simply sit in the tent and wait.

"Gun," Nine whispered, too loudly.

"I know," Four whispered. He retrieved the pistol

from his bedroll and loaded it as quietly as he could. He hid it in his belt, unzipped the tent and crawled out.

When he stood, he found he was among eight men, none of them known to him. These were not the red berets from earlier. These men wore mismatched uniforms and all carried outdated rifles and pistols.

"What is this about?" Four asked.

The leader of the men ignored Four and opened the tent door, thrusting his head in. He slashed his flashlight until he found Nine.

The speed with which Four and Nine were packed up, disarmed and put in the back of the pickup truck was remarkable. The tent was bunched together and thrown in the truck cab. Four had been able to indicate to the men that Nine was ill and could not sit up, so they laid him on the truckbed while Four sat above him on the wheel well. Two of the men sat in the truckbed with them, their guns lazily pointed into Nine's prone form.

The truck took off, back down the paved road. Four sat, exchanging glances with Nine, though he was sure neither of them knew what to do. Four's first instinct told him it was a simple police matter that would be resolved with a bribe. But there had been something outraged and personal about the men's attitude toward Nine that indicated this was not about money. The eight men had more the posture of a vigilante mob than the more businesslike ways of ransomers.

As they traveled through the humid night, despite himself Four found he could appreciate the astonishing smoothness of the road he'd paved. He half expected one of the men to express some kind of appreciation for it, too, but received no such praise. He watched the forest as it swam by. The sky above revealed no stars or moon.

The truck drove for nearly an hour before arriving at a break in the roadside forest, where they turned off onto a dirt road, deeply rutted by rain and seasonal streams. The truck shuddered and leaped and Nine's face was stiff, suppressing his agony. The truck was traveling far too fast for this kind of surface, and though Nine tried to be stoic, periodically the wheels dropped into a pothole and the truck plunged and rocked, and he let out an involuntary squeal.

They stopped in a small settlement of brick structures. The men piled out in front of what seemed to be a municipal building. It was marred by bullet holes and missing half of its roof. Human silhouettes moved through what looked to be a few sparsely furnished rooms. They took Nine first, carrying him carelessly through the front door, bending his body around the doorframe. Four was pushed to follow, his hands bound in front of him.

Inside there were five more men, two of whom were wearing civilian dress. A young man in green fatigues stood in the corner of the room, and at the desk sat a large, middle-aged man with a weary air. Behind silver-framed glasses his eyes were small and red ringed. His large hands were set on the rickety table in front of him. Part of the table's front-left leg was missing and had been replaced by a stack of canisters that looked to Four like land mines. Nine had been laid down just in front of the table, on the floor, between Four and the man.

"I am the commander here," the man at the desk said. From his uniform he seemed to be a rebel commander who now in peacetime had been given governing powers. Four had seen such men on this continent and others. They had no interest in the mundanity of governance; in the flush of international compassion and funds for rebuilding, they looked only to siphon enough for themselves to leave the country and send their children to private schools.

"There has been a complaint that this man has violated one of the women of this village," he said. "This is the woman's father." The commander pointed to an imposing man standing behind Four. His head was enormous, his eyebrows great black escarpments guarding his terrified eyes. Upon being referenced, he stood erect, his head tilted inquisitively as if posing for a picture but unsure how.

"Sir, this man is very sick," Four said.

"I see that he is," the commander said.

"He can't answer questions right now," Four explained. He knew he needed to slow down the proceedings, lest some violent act occur in the madness of haste and night. "The trouble of getting him here has weakened him. I wonder if we might allow him to rest until the morning?"

Four continued watching the woman's father. When the commander explained the situation, the father was oddly solicitous, as if the proceedings—bringing two foreigners to answer for the crime, one of them lying at his feet—had already exceeded his expectations, and that no delay could take away what he'd already achieved. He nodded gravely, his eyes near tears.

"Fine," said the commander.

XIX

WHEN FOUR WOKE, in a bunk bed in an adjoining room, the commander was exactly where he had been before, sitting at his desk. He was talking on a cell phone now, occasionally chuckling. Four could see the shoulder of an underfed guard in the doorway, his rifle pointing to the floor. There was a low windowframe on the wall near the commander's desk. In it there was no glass, only three rusted bars, and on the other side, three children in rags stood watching the room like spectators at the theater.

Four knelt down to check on Nine. He seemed to be asleep, but Four placed his finger under his nostrils to be sure. Feeling his feathery breath, he sat on his bunk again.

Throughout the morning, the commander made and received phone calls, and Four deduced he was weighing his options. Finally he entered the room.

"And how are you finding the accommodations?" he asked, and Four thought he might actually care.

"Can we get some water for my colleague?" Four asked.

The commander gave an order to the guard, who left languidly and then rattled through the building looking for a cup. As they waited, the commander's tone changed. "How is the road coming?"

"Good," Four said, then he thought he might leverage the project to speed up whatever process was unfolding in the police station. "But our schedule is very tight. We must continue as soon as possible. And with all due respect, our detention here is putting the timetable at risk. We have four days to have the road ready for the parade."

"The parade?" the commander asked. "There will be a parade? What sort of parade?"

Four paused. He had assumed the parade was a national event of great historical significance, something on par with an election or inauguration. But the fact that this commander knew nothing about it made him reconsider.

"To celebrate the road's completion," Four said. To blunt the force of this revelation, he added, "This is what

I was told at least. The road will open and the parade will christen it."

The commander seemed to find this logical and satisfactory, though there was a tightness in his mouth that indicated his displeasure at having no prior knowledge of it. The commander glanced at the children watching through the window and with a slash of his arm, shooed them away. They didn't move.

When the water arrived, ash-colored liquid in a soiled glass, Four dipped his shirt into it and brought it to Nine's lips. The water was unsafe to consume, so he only pretended to serve it to Nine.

"Is your friend able to speak now?" the commander asked.

Four glanced down at Nine, who closed his eyes in assent.

"No, he has not spoken in many days," Four said. "He doesn't expect to live."

The commander looked surprised and alarmed. "Is this true? What is the sickness?"

"Acute malaria. He hasn't responded to treatment. We were too late. Our assumption is that he already experienced liver failure. His skin has the jaundice."

"So why haven't you called for a plane?" the commander asked, sounding outraged by Four's indifference.

"We have," Four lied. "The company has refused."

The commander blinked quickly, taking this in. Four knew a rebel commander like this would see the logic in it, in the remorseless decisions necessary in the application of scarce resources. The children beyond the window watched intently.

"He has no family," Four added. He had adopted a resigned and businesslike tone, as if he had come to the same cold calculus himself—that Nine was not worth the money or trouble.

The sound of a motorcycle drawing closer overtook the room. The engine was cut and Four heard loud voices outside the building. The children left to see who it was, and one of the soldiers entered the room and spoke to the commander. The commander, perplexed and shocked by his conversation with Four, stood and seemed relieved to be able to divert his mind.

He left the room and moments later returned with a man following closely behind. It was Medallion. Medallion's eyes scanned the room.

"You are okay?"

Four told him they were fine. Remembering that he had said that Nine could not speak, he added, "He is no better. He still hasn't spoken. I think it's just a matter of time." They both looked to Nine's gray visage, and Four and Medallion were able to exchange the most fleeting of glances as they both turned back to the commander.

"Sir," Medallion said. He approached the commander and took his hand lightly. They left the room to have a private discussion while Four and Nine stared at each other silently. Nine's eyes were mirthful, the first time Four had seen this kind of light in Nine's face in many days.

When Medallion returned, alone, he sat next to Four on the bunk. "Because he knows"—he winked almost imperceptibly—"that Nine is dying, things are changed. If he was a healthy man, this would be a complicated situation. There would be a trial, and Nine would be imprisoned. Perhaps made to marry the young woman. But in this situation, the commander suggests a payment to compensate for the ruin of the young woman. Do you have your money with you?"

"I do."

"May I see what you have?"

Four reached into his shoe and removed the folded bills. They were wet with perspiration, but Medallion took no notice. He removed two bills from the bunch and put them in his own pocket. Medallion stared at the remaining bills. "This will have to do," he said. "May I take this?"

Four allowed Medallion to return to the commander with the money. Almost immediately he heard the commander's barking negotiations. The commander was outraged by the paltry sum, which would have to be split between the wet-eyed father and the commander, but Medallion eventually calmed him. And then came to retrieve Four and Nine.

"We are done."

XX

THE OXCART MEDALLION had hired smelled of
manure and human urine. It was taking Four and Nine
back to the RS-80 as Medallion rode alongside on his
motorcycle.

Nine's eyes were closed tight. The road was the one
Four had paved, but the wheels of the oxcart were roughly
hewn and the cart shook and shimmied.

"I'm sorry," Four said to him.

"That went far better than I expected," Medallion
said, and laughed. Four smiled. Nine had been arrested
while gravely ill, Four's money was gone, and they'd used
the last of their funds to hire an oxcart. But they were
alive and free.

"The fact that the commander negotiated with me at
all was remarkable. He is of the other faction," Medallion
said. He seemed to be contemplating the strangeness of

this. "But he no doubt suspected you had money, and would spend it quickly to get your companion out of prison." Again he paused, as if unraveling what had happened. "The commander wanted a transaction. My guess is that he will split the fee you paid with the father and he will forget about the incident. The father, though—I don't know. I fear for the safety of his daughter. Because she is spoiled, she could be killed or might kill herself now. Many women do this."

When they returned to the vehicle, a dawn of pale green was breaking. They found Cousin and two other men gathered around the machine. The men helped move Nine from the oxcart, and the oxcart driver went on his way, traveling south on the bright black road.

"You have been up all night. We can leave you to rest," Medallion said to Four.

But Four felt strangely awake. He knew that the schedule was now indeed in jeopardy, and he sensed that there might be other distractions before they reached the capital.

"I'm starting again now," he said.

He couldn't waste the day, or even half the day. He took food from his pack and loaded it into the vehicle. Medallion directed the men to lift Nine and arrange him again on the hood of the paver. They assembled his makeshift bedding and strapped him fast to the frame.

"I would assist you today," Medallion said, "but I must return to my wife. Cousin will be clearing the road for you today. I will see you in the capital. I will bring my wife in the tuk-tuk. When you are high in the Imperial Hotel, look for us. The tuk-tuk has a bright yellow roof. That will be us."

Four started the RS-80 and the engine sent a vibration through the frame. Four saw, emerging from the sarcophagus on the hood, Nine's outstretched hand. Nine turned his wrist slowly, an homage to royalty. He was ready.

Four started down the road.

After an hour he saw a bright silver roof of corrugated steel. It was far larger than any structure he'd seen since he'd arrived. A roof like this was rare in this country; he assumed the building was both new and built by people with means. Indeed, as he drew closer, he saw that it was an NGO, one he had not heard of. As the RS-80 passed slowly, he saw staff moving in and out of the building. One man, in a khaki suit, left the building and got into a gleaming white Range Rover and, without acknowledging Four, drove up the embankment and onto the just-paved highway, speeding south on it as if it had been finished for years, not minutes.

The settlements became denser and more modernized. Planes and helicopters were more frequent, and traffic on the road more chaotic. Vehicles approached from every side and used the road behind him and in front without regard for the work at hand. Fewer trees dotted the landscape, and fires from homes and businesses sent twisting plumes of white smoke into the azure sky. Passersby waved to Four and he occasionally waved back. He was exhausted and was ready to be finished. His screen said he was two pods from the end. When he reached the next one, he had three minutes while the RS-80 put the new pod into place, so he closed his eyes. Instantly sleep took him under.

He woke to the signal that the new pod was in place. He opened his eyes to find a trio of women in colorful dresses at his window. They had a basket with them, and were pointing to it, and to Nine. Four could not imagine how they knew Nine was there amid the bundle.

He opened his window. One of the women roared a string of unintelligible words. She had a high forehead and wore a bright turquoise wrap that reached her ankles. Again she gestured to Nine, and to the basket, in which she seemed to have a mortar and pestle. She yelled more, spittle gathering around her tense mouth.

The RS-80 was ready to move. Four smiled and waved the women off, and allowed the machine to move forward. But the women did not disperse. They simply moved to the side, like water parting, and walked alongside the vehicle.

Four waved them off again, but they were no longer paying him attention. Instead they talked among themselves, seeming to be debating a course of action. Finally the youngest and smallest of the women, in an orange dress with a shorter cut, took a plastic spoon from the basket and filled it with a dark paste from the pestle.

Again Four waved her off, but the woman in orange paid him no mind. She stepped quickly onto the chassis of the RS-80 and leaned over to Nine's head. She reached in, folding the bedding back to reveal his face. Now Four could see his eyes open as she placed her hand on his forehead with calm authority. With the other hand, she brought the spoon to his mouth and split his lips with her fingers. The paste went in and she closed his mouth, helping him to swallow it.

All of this happened too quickly for Four to do anything about it. Something about their deliberate speed, the surety of their mission, had paralyzed him, had lulled him into believing they were acquaintances of Medallion who were offering food, gifts. Now this nimble young woman had fed Nine something and was already back on the side of the road, reporting her success to the other two women. The three of them ceased keeping pace with the vehicle, breaking off and blending back into the shops along the road. Four looked behind him, and found the one in turquoise waving to him in a way that was final.

He turned back to Nine, whose face was no longer visible. The woman in orange had moved Nine's bedding. Four's first instinct was to stop the vehicle, to investigate Nine, to take whatever was left in his mouth and scrape it out—to shut down the machine and send Nine back to the clinic they had recently passed.

But there was something in the women's way, their businesslike manner, that led him to think proceeding was the best and indeed only option. They had given him some kind of local food, some kind of medicine, so what, he thought. He knew so little about the people of this region, but certainly there were not among them a trio of female assassins administering poisons in the light of day.

XXI

WHEN FOUR POWERED down the paver that afternoon, he found Nine awake and smiling. There was color in his face, and when he saw Four, his eyes welled. "My savior," he said.

With some difficulty Four lowered Nine from the hood of the paver and dragged him to the side of the road. He brushed aside some gravel and arranged Nine so his head looked down the gentle grade. Once settled, Nine took Four's arm with remarkable strength.

"My superior," Nine said, and smiled.

Four went to the vehicle to retrieve his pack. He returned and threw a nutrition bar to Nine. Its plastic wrapper made a scraping sound against the plastic tarp still enclosing Nine.

"Will we make the schedule?" Nine asked.

"We'll be done tomorrow."

"Where's the man? The helper?"

"He's coming. When the road's done he's bringing his wife for treatment. At the hospital in the city."

"So we did something good," Nine said. "You did, that is. We actually did something here. I've been picturing the parade and it makes me proud. You happy?"

"I don't know," Four said. He had been thinking about Medallion and his wife, and when he thought about people like that, quickly reaching the capital and its promises, he felt some satisfaction.

"I'm sorry, though," Nine said. "I know I didn't do much to *mitigate obstacles*."

Nine smiled as if the two of them had established a wonderful inside joke. Four could not pretend he had forgiveness for Nine.

"You should not do this kind of work again," he said.

"I know," Nine said. "I see that now. I do. I watched you. You just do the work. You don't look left or right. "

Four softened toward Nine. "You gave away the first-aid kit, didn't you?"

Nine nodded, almost imperceptibly.

"And the satellite phone?"

Nine looked into his open palms. "I thought they needed them more than we did."

Four was unaffected. Nothing surprised him and none of this mattered now. It was over and he was going home. He pictured himself on the ferry, passing his archipelago's whaleback stones, seeing his family waiting for him on the landing. "I'm going to rest awhile before dinner," Four said, and moved to retrieve his earphones.

Nine raised himself to his side. "Can I ask what you listen to when you put those in? Even when I'm close, I don't hear any music."

Normally Four would not allow a stranger, and he considered Nine a stranger, to hear his recording. But soon he would leave this country and leave Nine, and would never see him again. He gave Nine his earphones and looked away.

"Sounds like a kitchen," Nine said, listening intently. "Plates and silverware being set." Four had not expected Nine to narrate what he heard, but he found it oddly pleasant.

"A child's voice. That must be your daughter. You have a daughter. You told me you weren't married. But of course you're married. Of course you have a child. That explains so much. Her voice! It's funny how high it is. It sounds like a cartoon. What's she saying over and over?"

Four knew the word was *breakfast*. It was his

daughter's favored time of day. She was so quick to rise. When she opened her eyes in the morning she was wholly awake, on her feet, moving, as if she'd been only pretending to sleep through all the dark hours.

"Now a quick wet clicking," Nine continued. "I'm thinking eggs being whisked in a bowl?" Yes, Four thought, exactly. "Now someone's humming. A woman. That must be your wife. She has a pretty voice. Is that a song? It sounds familiar."

Four pictured his wife uncapping his daughter's cup, the spillproof one she could hold with her tiny hand.

Nine's eyes opened wide. "Wow. A loud banging. What is that? Sounds like a woodpecker."

As soon as his daughter's cup was filled with her carrot juice, she banged it like an exultant king. His wife would calmly ask her to stop, and she would, taking a long pull of juice and wiping her mouth with the back of her hand. She was a brazen and unflinching child, having never been made aware of the vulnerabilities of her flesh.

"Now the eggs are simmering," Nine said. "Now a sound like chopping. Someone's chopping something."

Apples, melon, celery. Four would cut them and his wife would arrange the pieces in a radial for their daughter, who would put her cup in the middle of them and stare, as if momentarily stunned by their beautiful symmetry. Then, with a heavy sigh, she would take the first spoke from the wheel and eat it.

"Hm. Just sounds of silverware. Tinking. How long does this tape go on?"

XXII

AS THEY APPROACHED the capital, Nine was now squeezed into the cab. The forest gave way to shantytowns that stitched themselves into waves of blue-tented internally displaced camps and then stone dwellings hundreds of years old. And soon all the settlements knelt before the city, itself an irrational mix of ancient and modern, glass and iron and wood.

"Look," Nine said.

Behind them, stretching as far as they could see, people from the south were on the new highway, making their way toward the gleaming city. There were the ill and infirm, carried on oxcarts and pulled by bicycles. There were pickup trucks bearing produce. There was a line of women pulling wagons full of woven goods. All were moving at the pace of the paver, as if respectfully following a funeral procession.

"See this?" Nine said. "They're waiting for us to finish. Don't you see? It's like a parade before the real parade. This is one of hope. A procession of longing. The second we're done, their world catapults into the twenty-first century. Trade, medical care, access to government services, information, education, relatives, electricity and the northern port."

Somewhere back there were Medallion and his wife, Four assumed. They had not made arrangements to say goodbye, but Four owed him much, and Nine owed him more.

The last few kilometers were chaotic. As they entered the city, some of the people from the south peeled off into the city's streets and alleys. There was trading to be done, people to meet. In a few instances there seemed to be tensions. Some watchers on the roadside stood and spat words at the people from the south. But that seemed to be a minority of the audience gathered. The rest of them were actively cheering the finishing of the road. Children played on it, twirling, running, watching their elastic shadows.

At the road's end there were flags and banners, a thousand soldiers in uniform, all gathered at a wide staging ground at the edge of the city. Beyond, the glass high-rises of the city's waterfront shone gold in the afternoon sun. This city was a hundred years ahead of the town from which they'd begun the road. Four knew that gap would quickly collapse now. He'd seen it happen before.

His work ended suddenly. The road ceased short of the city center; they would add on-ramps later. When he'd reached the end, Four powered down the RS-80, ceding it to the same two mechanics who had delivered it two weeks before. An array of personages and local police swept Four and Nine from the vehicle to a reception area, where they met various dignitaries and commanders, all of them in a jovial but businesslike mood. There was talk that the president might appear to shake their hands, but finally they were told he was too busy with last-minute plans. Four and Nine were feted and fed and late that night were escorted to the hotel called the Imperial, where they were given adjoining suites with views of the city and of the road they'd finished.

Four should have felt tired, and should have slept for days, but that night his mind could not rest. He turned on the television and watched what must have been archival footage of the government army conducting exercises. He retrieved his earphones, settled them into his ears and arranged himself in bed, then pressed play. He was asleep before his daughter began banging her cup.

XXIII

"YOU'RE NOT STAYING for the parade?" Nine asked.

"I can't. I'd planned to be home by now," Four said. "My family's waiting."

"But we were on time," Nine said.

"Yes, but I expected to be early," Four said. "You'll stay?" Four asked.

"I'll stay," Nine said. "Maybe for a week, just to soak it in. Get a free meal here and there."

They looked down at the road below. It was pristine, so black and lightless it looked like a chasm.

"Quiet, though, isn't it?" Nine noted. "Yesterday there were ten thousand people on it."

"They're just getting ready for the parade, I imagine," Four said. "And I'm sure they need the road clear so they can begin without obstruction."

When Four got to the airport, it, too, was oddly quiet.

176

The company had found Four a place on a luxurious jet, and Four had no interactions with customs officials of any kind. He was driven to the tarmac by a uniformed official and walked up the stairs carrying only the pack he'd had with him the last two weeks. He had acquired nothing and lost nothing.

On board, he found himself among a group of formally dressed men and women, some of them local, more of them visitors like himself. He walked down the aisle, ignored by all of the passengers but one, a man who was smiling at him as he passed. It took Four a moment to place him. It was the rebel general who had approached him on the highway. He was in civilian dress now, but was wearing the mirrored sunglasses, round and bright like two full moons, that Four had seen hanging from his uniform when they'd met. Four nodded to him and took his seat.

As the plane taxied and took off, the passengers pressed their faces to the windows, preoccupied with what was happening below. For a group of experienced travelers, they were acting like children on their first flight.

The parade, Four realized. As the plane circled low around the city, they jostled to see the parade. He laughed at himself, at his ability to temporarily forget something he'd made possible. For a moment the plane followed the path of the road, and Four saw it clearly, the straight line he'd made between north and south. Thousands of southerners were making their way toward the capital on foot and in small vehicles. They would be joining the parade, or meeting it, he assumed. With a start he remembered that Medallion had said he would be among those following the new highway to the capital. He searched for Medallion's tuk-tuk with the yellow roof, and finally, amid a throng of walkers and a few dull-colored cars, he was sure he found it. His eyes welled and he smiled, to think how simple it could all be, cause and effect in a place like this. Then a gasp came from a passenger in front of him.

"Oh lord," she said.

Four looked down to see what seemed to be a line of trucks leaving the parade's staging grounds. The trucks were military-style personnel carriers, and emerged from the hangars around the highway's end, six of them, side by side, then twelve, in tight configuration. Then a dozen more, followed by a line of jeeps and trucks with mounted guns. Finally a fleet of tanks appeared and followed the convoy in rigid formation. Soldiers on foot embroidered the parade on either side of the road.

When the procession met the pilgrims walking to the capital, the soldiers opened fire and the people were cut down like tall grass meeting a scythe's blade. Four, sitting in a plane slowly banking away, could hear nothing from this height. But the people continued to fall, the yellow tuk-tuk ceased its advance, was crushed silently under tank tread, and the convoy continued unimpeded down the immaculate road.

ACKNOWLEDGMENTS

Thank you JJ, ZH, SM and all at Knopf. Thank you AW. Thank you JR. Thank you Em-J, AU, CS, ZS and DG. Thank you OVG, HM, KG, CM and SP. Thank you VAD and MA. Thank you UN and ACLU and MSV and IRC. Thank you without abbreviation VV.